Finding Home

FINDING HOME

Jon West

ISBN 979-8-89416-023-8 (Hardcover)
ISBN 979-8-89416-022-1 (Paperback)
ISBN 979-8-89416-024-5 (Audiobook)
ISBN 979-8-89416-021-4 (eBook)

Copyright © 2024 Jon West

All rights reserved.

No part of this publication may be reproduced, stored in or introduced into a retrieval system, or transmitted, in any form, or by any means (electrical, mechanical, photocopying, recording or otherwise) without the prior written permission of the copyright owner, except for the use of brief quotations in a book review.

To request permission, contact the publisher at requests@folk.studio

Published by
FOLK STUDIO 451
San Antonio, Texas
https://folk.studio

This book is dedicated to the greatest storyteller of all time, my father. Through his tales, he wove us into our family lore, past, present, and future. He will always live in the hearts and minds of all who knew him. Thanks, Dad.

—Jon West

CONTENTS

Chapter I   The Praters 1

Chapter II   The Whitaker Home 9

Chapter III   Milo 12

Chapter IV   Gladys 20

Chapter V   Richard Elliott Standish, Esq. 32

Chapter VI   The Calling 37

Chapter VII   New York City 41

Chapter VIII   The Journey 46

Chapter IX   The Good Father 52

Chapter X   Dianna Sue 61

Chapter XI   Koen Van Haaften 67

Chapter XII   Ada 77

Chapter XIII   Marlow 83

Chapter XIV   Cyrus Smith 87

Chapter XV   Betty and Freddy 102

Chapter XVI   Evelynn 107

Chapter XVII   The Glasby's 113

Chapter XVIII   Christmas Day 119

Chapter XIX   Finding Home 138

FORWARD

At the dawn of the 20th century, the world teetered on the edge of transformation. The roar of steam engines, the clatter of telegraphs, and the whir of new machines promised progress—but for many, it came with a cost. It was a time of great upheaval, where old ways gave way to the new, and individuals were left to navigate the unknown: to reconcile their pasts, adapt to a shifting present, and forge futures brimming with possibility. *Finding Home* is the story of such a journey—an odyssey that mirrors the heartbeat of an era.

At its core, *Finding Home* is more than a tale of one boy's trials and triumphs. It is a testament to resilience, to love found in unexpected places, and to the human need for connection even in the face of loss. Jasper P. Whittington III is not just a character; he is a reflection of countless souls at the turn of the century—individuals caught between the old world and the promise of the new. Through Jasper's eyes, we experience the sweeping plains, the thundering locomotives, and the spirit of invention that defined this pivotal moment in history.

As readers, we are invited not just to follow Jasper's journey, but to reflect on our own. *Finding Home* reminds us that even the hardest roads lead somewhere beautiful. That the struggles we endure shape us. And that sometimes, "home" is not a place, but the people we choose to love and the stories we carry with us.

So open this book, and step into a time of change, a world of promise, and a story that will stay with you long after you turn the last page. Jasper's odyssey awaits, and it just might inspire you to look at your own journey with new eyes.

Welcome to *Finding Home.*

CHAPTER I
The Praters

May 31st, 1897

On Sundays, Elisabeth and Lottie Prater always arrived early at Marlow First Christian Church to place fresh flowers in the sanctuary before the morning service. On this occasion, as they approached the entrance, they noticed a woven basket at the door. Sounds of cooing and small grunts were coming from it. Nine-year-old Lottie raced to the basket to look inside. There lay a newborn baby boy wrapped in dirty rags and newspapers.

"Mommy, Mommy! It's a baby! We found a baby! Can we keep him?" Lottie's heart poured out.

"Land sakes! What is this?" said Elisabeth. Reaching down for the infant, she noticed a torn piece of paper pinned to the lip of the basket. Jasper P. Whittington III was scribbled on it. "Now, who would abandon a baby like this?"

Her eyes welled with tears when she silently answered her question. Oklahoma Territory was not forgiving of young women who were in an unfortunate way. Leaving an infant at the door of a church was a common and heartbreaking last option for some young unwed mothers wanting to save their baby's life. "Can we keep him? He needs us! Oh, look how beautiful he is! He's perfect! I'm going to name him Basil, after Daddy!"

"He already has a name, sugar," Elisabeth said, looking at the paper. "And remember, he's one of God's children, not a puppy. Let's take him home, feed him, and clean him up. We'll talk to Daddy about it."

She was already falling in love with the baby, but Elisabeth was a pragmatic prairie woman. She already had Lottie and the two boys at home, and her family was just getting by.

"Land sakes," she whispered.

They gathered up the little boy, placed the fresh flowers in the church, and began the walk home. As they started down the red dirt road, Lottie insisted on carrying the basket but only managed a block until her Mama took over. They completed the remaining three blocks, and by the time the girls got to their front yard, there was a gaggle of neighbor ladies flocking around the baby. A decision was made to feed and clean him up and then discuss options for him. The ladies went home and prepared lunch for their families. They would meet back at the Prater home for tea in the afternoon.

Mother and daughter entered the home through the kitchen. As they walked through the door, the baby boy wailed from hunger and discomfort. Basil Pitt Prater (B.P.) was watering the barn's livestock (a milk cow and a few chickens) when he heard the cries.

"What the hell was that?" mumbled B.P. He put down the water bucket and headed for the house as the crying continued.

After removing his boots and hanging up his hat, he entered the kitchen and saw his wife and daughter tending to a baby while water was being heated on the stove.

"Lizzy, what do we have here?" he asked.

"This boy was left at the church's front door, Basil. After lunch, the ladies are stopping by to discuss what needs to be done for the baby's sake."

"So you ladies are gonna find a home for it?" asked B.P. as he rubbed his forehead.

"Basil Pitt Prater, he needs a washing, food, and affection. I assume a good Christian man like yourself would be eager to help this child."

"Oh no . . ." said B.P. as he exhaled.

"Mr. Prater, what are you on about?" Lizzy asked as she fastened a new diaper on the infant.

"When you refer to me as a 'Good Christian,' it either costs me money or a good night's sleep!"

Elisabeth and his daughter stopped what they were doing and blankly stared at him. B.P. cautiously backed out of the kitchen and resumed his chores.

To the women on the street, "in the afternoon" meant one thirty p.m. sharp. It was time enough to feed the family, wash up, and see their men off to the mill, where they would share their stories and a bottle. As the women filed into Lizzy's parlor, Lottie offered them tea and biscuits. She was learning to be a gracious hostess and could proudly balance the plate of cookies without one landing on the floor.

After a barrage of compliments and kind nods, the business at hand was breached. Any woman in the group would take in this sleeping boy as their own, but they were also aware of the consequences. It would be a significant burden for any family on their street, both financially and emotionally.

"The Whitaker family has opened an orphan's home near Tulsa. This is just the circumstance it was established for," said Ophelia Ottman as she rocked the child.

The Whitaker Home for Wayward Children was established in 1897 by W.T. and Stacy Whitaker to provide a home for orphaned white children of the Indian Territory.

"I'll talk to the judge about it tomorrow," said Laura Nicole, the courthouse administration secretary. "We just received some new application forms from the Whitaker Trust Fund."

"How long of a process is it?" asked Elisabeth.

"Oh, shouldn't take more than a week," answered Laura.

"Well, we have ample food and time for him 'til all is arranged. We'll keep the boy here while you take care of the paperwork," said Elizabeth as she cleared the teacups.

All the other ladies nodded and agreed.

After all the technical business was finished, it was time to pass around the baby. The parlor was aglow with love and affection for the boy, and all the adoring women gently held him and spoke to him only as mothers could.

Little Jasper was a lovely child to care for. He would never outright cry and had a perpetual smile. He even slept all night, sharing a room with Lottie. Since there was no crib, they emptied Lottie's bottom dresser drawer and made a bed for him there. On the third morning, Lizzy went to Lottie's room and found Jasper missing. Her heart skipped a beat as she began searching the house for the child. As she entered the kitchen, she saw B.P. nursing him with a warm bottle.

"Do you miss it?" Lizzy asked. She smiled and slipped her arm around his shoulders as they watched Jasper empty the bottle.

"Yeah, but not enough to have another baby. I swear! He's as sweet as cotton candy."

Elisabeth walked to the stove and started coffee and breakfast. She added a few chunks of coal to the low glowing ambers and fanned them. Within half an hour, the sleepy-eyed children had gathered at the kitchen table, hungry and eager to start their day. The twin boys were in the first grade, and Lottie was in her final year, fourth grade. Children in small rural communities didn't have the luxury of a complete education. Childhood ended with the fourth grade. Their families needed them to keep farms and households running.

After breakfast, B.P. went into town to rent a mule to plow a new garden, and the kids headed to school. A knock and a "Yoo-hoo!" came through the Prater's screen door.

"Come on in, Laura! We're in the kitchen," yelled Lizzy.

Laura entered and found Lizzy changing Jasper's diaper. He was smiling ear to ear when a little fountain of tinkle shot up, set off by the cool air. Both women laughed out loud at the sight.

"I spoke to the sheriff. He will inform as many law agencies as possible about Jasper to see if they can find a relative who can take him in. I have everything regarding the Wayward Home paperwork, and it seems fairly easy. We could fill it out together." The women shared a silent moment of sadness, their hearts torn, knowing Jasper was headed to an institution.

"Well, at least it's a private institution, unlike those horrid state-run orphanages. He'll be fine. Who knows? Maybe a family member will see the notifications and claim him," said Laura. Lizzy couldn't speak for fear of crying.

"We shall pray for him and put our faith in the good Lord!" said Laura, holding back her own tears.

Four days later, B.P. was waiting on platform one at the Marlow train station. The neighborhood womenfolk were all around him, crying and passing Jasper around for a last goodbye kiss. B.P. had been told to meet with a nurse from the orphanage at the train station in Oklahoma City to turn Jasper over.

The nurse would then take the boy to Pryor, just outside Tulsa, to The Whitaker Home for Wayward Children.

The train's steam whistle blew and the conductor announced, "All aboard for Chickasha, Norman, and OKC!"

B.P. took Jasper in his arms along with a knotted handkerchief packed with a cheese sandwich and an apple. Elisabeth looked into her husband's eyes and tearfully whispered, "See ya at suppertime, honey." B.P. acknowledged her with a wink and a smile. As he turned to board the train, he heard the tearful good-byes come from all the ladies. He didn't dare turn to say anything for fear of showing his own tears.

With a blast of steam, the train released its brakes and slowly chugged north. B.P. took a last look at the women on the platform, tightly huddled together and crying. It was gonna be a tough week.

Now in Oklahoma City, B.P. Prater tipped his hat and smiled at the nurse holding young Jasper. "All aboard! Norman, Chickasha, Marlow, and Duncan," shouted the conductor from platform four.

"Thank you, Mr. Prater, for taking the time to bring us little Jasper," said Nurse Suffring. "We shall be sure to pass on to his future parents how much you and your family cared for him. May the good Lord bless and watch over you and yours."

"Thank you, ma'am," he said. He gave the cooing baby one more pinch on the cheek and smiled, then turned and boarded the train.

B.P.'s emotions were a tangled mess as the train lurched forward. As minutes became hours, he rehashed the conversations that had led them to this point. He felt they were doing the right thing for the boy, but wondered if they could have taken him in. Maybe they could have made room for him. He wasn't THAT much trouble. But he'd get a better education at the wayward home. And with the twins, a new baby might have driven Lizzy crazy, "taking me with her," he mumbled, shaking his head. As far as money went, you didn't have to look far to find a more stable financial situation than theirs. But babies needed more than money.

"Dammit!" he said aloud as the whistle blew and the train clattered down the tracks toward home.

CHAPTER II
The Whitaker Home

September 14th, 1908

Eleven-year-old Jasper sat quietly with the other sixteen children in The Whitaker Home for Wayward Children's community room. It was his favorite room, where he spent most of his free time. He frequently picked books from its vast collection and would spend hours reading alone. He loved reading Dickens but also enjoyed new authors like H.G. Wells. This was the only home Jasper knew. He had seen scores of kids come and go over his lifetime and knew that the longer you stayed, the less likely you'd be adopted. Jasper had the longest tenure of all the kids and most of the staff. He had long since given up being adopted and focused on his studies. He was always at the top of the class in school, and his education had already far surpassed anyone in Marlow. He wanted to become a doctor.

An unscheduled announcement was to be made, so the whole school gathered in the main room. Jasper was excited. Nothing new or different ever happened here, so this must be big. "Maybe we're getting some goats or even a horse!" he thought.

An elderly man and woman sat at the front of the room, silently watching the quiet, well-behaved children. The woman occasionally wiped her eyes with a lace handkerchief as her husband patted her hand. The door behind the kids softly opened and closed. Silently, Miss Derickson walked past them to the front of the gathering and stood next to the older couple. She had never looked so disheveled. "Whatever could it be?" thought Jasper.

"Children, I'd like to introduce you to Mr. and Mrs. W.T. Whitaker." Miss Derickson's voice quivered. The elderly man stood, looked into the children's faces, and began to speak.

"This home was established after Mrs. Whitaker and I lost our son, Callahan. He was taken by bandits and never seen again." Mrs. Whitaker had her face in her hands as her tears flowed freely. "We wanted, under the good Lord's guidance, to give other children opportunities our son was deprived of. Looking in your faces now, I know we've done God's work."

"Last year, Oklahoma became America's 46th state. It's the beginning of a new era. As American citizens, you children will now be in the care of the great state of Oklahoma." Mrs. Whitaker sobbed, never raising her face from her hands. Mr. Whitaker's gaze moved across the rows of stunned children staring back at him. He opened his mouth to speak but then only cleared his throat and coughed, turned, and sat next to his heartbroken wife to give her comfort. The room was silent but for Mrs. Whitaker's weeping.

Miss Derickson readdressed the children. "Starting Monday, this home will be renamed The Oklahoma State Home. You are welcome to remain with us until you're adopted or until your eighteenth birthday. The children arriving from this point on will be released on or about their fourteenth birthday. Other than that, everything will remain the same."

The sadness in the staff's eyes only fueled the children's fear as they sat, reeling from the news. These kids all understood the feeling of abandonment, and they were feeling it now. They couldn't understand the politics that was changing their lives. They only knew that the security of a forever home was gone.

"Any questions?" Miss Derickson asked. The absence of any question at all spoke volumes. Without putting it in words, they knew their lives had taken a turn for the worse.

Over the next three years, the home began to erode. The number of kids staying there grew from twenty-five to a hundred and twenty-five. The state paid the orphanage per child, but the prior level of comfort, care, and guidance was impossible to maintain. Kids weren't being adopted. So the goal for most children and the staff was to leave and never return.

First to disappear were the books Jasper loved so much, along with the paintings of the Whitaker family. The old portraits had inspired him. He had looked deeply into the paintings, imagining he was part of their family. Now he was angry at himself for even thinking that. "You're on your own, an orphan, nothing else," he thought.

CHAPTER III
Milo

May 19th, 1911

At the age of fourteen, Jasper had had enough. Meat was now served only once a week, if that. Older children were now hired out as day laborers, picking cotton, peanuts, and other cash crops. Many of the boys sent out for work had not returned.

Jasper didn't need to sneak off. He was legally old enough to strike out on his own. That morning, with no pretense, he stood from the breakfast table and walked out the front door with only the clothes on his back. Not a single protest came from the staff. There was no fear or insecurity in his heart. Only the satisfaction of never seeing the State Home again. He was breathing the air of a free man, and it felt good.

In ten minutes he reached the main gate on Highway 69, where he stopped and pondered his next move. Jasper had never been off the property and had no idea which direction to go. He knew nothing of life away from the home. He had not been recruited to work on nearby farms, nor did he ever volunteer. He'd always just kept himself busy tending the school's livestock.

BOOM-CLACKER-CLACKER-BOOM, BOOM!

"What the heck is that?" thought Jasper. The biggest machine he'd ever seen was about a quarter of a mile away, coming around the bend, rolling towards him. He had heard the other boys talk about big, noisy machines but had never witnessed one. This one appeared to be the size of a barn! A man stood in the middle of the machine, tugging and moving different levers.

Jasper was dumbfounded as the mechanical monster rolled up to him and shut down. "Morning!" came from the friendly face, looking down at the befuddled fourteen-year-old.

"What in tarnation is that?" asked Jasper.

"This here is a 1911 Two-Speed Gear Drive International Harvester 12 Horsepower Type A Tractor. I'm Milo Clemmens."

"I'm Jasper P. Whittington III. What's it for?" asked Jasper, his eyes still fixed on the tractor.

"I'm using it for wheat harvest. It does the work of five men. What's the P. stand for?"

"Nothing. Just P," answered Jasper.

"Whatcha doing out here, boy?" Milo asked, smiling.

It took Jasper a moment to compose himself and get past his first encounter with a self-propelled contraption. "I'm leaving that State Home. I'm striking out on my own, like Huckleberry Finn. It's within my rights," Jasper said.

"Well, what's your intention, son?" asked Milo.

"Don't rightly know, sir," Jasper said, looking down the road.

"I'm headed into town to fill up with petrol. Why don't you ride with me, and we'll talk it over?" Milo suggested.

"I'd be much obliged, sir," said Jasper, approaching the machine.

"You see that big wheel in front of you?" Milo pointed.

"This one?" asked Jasper, placing his hand on a large iron wheel on the side of the engine.

"That's it! It's called a balancer. Spin it clockwise till you hear a bang. Then step back," instructed Milo.

As Jasper spun the wheel, Milo turned on the magneto, pulled out the choke, and advanced the throttle.

BANG! chugga, chagga, BANG! Jasper's eyes got wide as coffee saucers and he asked, "Is it supposed to do that?"

"Atta girl!" Milo smiled and patted the tractor, then motioned to Jasper, "Climb on up and stand next to me."

Jasper crawled up and joined him. His heart was about to pound out of his chest. Milo set the throttle on full, and soon they were moving at the brisk pace of six miles per hour. All Jasper could do was laugh.

Within an hour, Milo and Jasper were rolling into the outskirts of Pryor. The loud tractor could be heard from a mile away – stirring the people out of their little townhomes. The tractor was still quite a sight for the townspeople. As the machine passed they stood in their yards and waved to Milo and Jasper. Milo returned the waves and smiled.

Jasper was dumbfounded. People had their own properties and gardens and looked just like the families in the novels he had read.

Milo and Jasper pulled up to the single gas pump at Martin's General Store in front of the courthouse. Steam escaped from the water-fill cap as Milo shut off the magneto. The engine was a bit reluctant but complied with a sputter and bang, then fell silent.

Wide-eyed, Jasper studied the busy town center. He'd only experienced towns in books. Now he actually saw, felt, and smelled one for the first time. "Land sakes!" he muttered.

Jasper's reactions touched Milo. He now realized this boy had never been off the farm. "Wait here, son, I need to fetch some water," he said, stepping down and reaching for a water bucket.

"I'll get it, Mr. Clemmens!" blurted Jasper, taking the bucket from him.

"There's a spigot over there by the watering trough," Milo pointed out. "Bring that funnel, too." Jasper ran to the fixture and filled the bucket.

Alain Martin, a French immigrant, owned the store. He walked out to greet Milo.

"Who do we have here, Mr. Clemmens?" asked Alain, extending a hand.

"That is Jasper P. Whittington III. He's on his life's first adventure," said Milo, shaking Alain's hand.

"Pleased to meet you, sir!" said Jasper, extending his hand to Alain.

"Jasper, Mr. Martin and I have been doing business for years. You'll be working with him while you're working for me," said Milo.

"Working for you?" asked Jasper.

"Son, how do you expect to take on a proper adventure without any money?" Milo asked.

"Oh . . . well, I haven't planned that far ahead," said Jasper meekly. The two men smiled at his response.

"Aw! The impetuous youth!" said Alain, shaking his head. "You remind me of me when I first came to America."

"I reckon that was your big adventure, Mr. Martin," said Jasper.

"Just one of many, my boy."

"Are you from France?" asked Jasper.

"What do you know of France?" asked Alain.

"Just what I've read in books. There was a revolution, like here, in America. They also eat snails!" said Jasper.

"Well, some folks do," smiled Mr. Martin.

"The home I grew up in had a huge library, and I made a point of reading every book I could. Jules Verne is an amazing author! He's from France. Twenty Thousand Leagues Under the Sea is one of my favorites."

Mr. Martin paused. Most people in Pryor never made it past fourth grade. This boy was educated.

"Are all the children at the home well educated?" asked Mr. Martin.

"Not anymore, sir. After the state took over, they took out the big library and left some magazines and pulps. When new ones arrived, I read them in a day. They weren't as good as the books, but they were something."

"But what about school?" asked Alain.

"They only have school until the fourth grade now," Jasper answered. "I'm way past that!"

"You damn sure are," said Milo, studying Jasper's face.

"Show me where to put this water, Mr. Clemmens," said Jasper, nodding toward the bucket.

"Not now, son. The radiator is too hot. We got to let her cool down, or you'll get scalded," said Milo. "Why don't you head into the store and have a look around?"

Jasper's face lighted up. "Yes, sir!"

Jasper entered the store with reverence and caution. He stopped two steps inside the door. The sights and smells were incredible! Behind the counter there were canned goods, dry goods, candies, hats and boots, and small medicine bottles. Looking towards the back, he saw shelves loaded with books!

"Man alive!" Jasper said aloud. Hearing him, the two men at the gas pump laughed. He walked slowly to the books and read the titles. They were mostly Western dime novels. His reading ability far exceeded the level these were written for. But they were books! Without even looking at the titles, he grabbed three and strolled back to the pump. He thought this would be enough for a couple of days.

"Jasper, where you headed with Mr. Martin's books?" asked Milo.

"I should have them finished in a day or so. Then I'll bring them back to swap out for some others," responded Jasper.

The answer froze Mr. Martin.

"That's not how it works, son. You need to pay for the books before you take them. Then they're your books. Then you can take them home," said Mr. Clemmens.

"Oh. Well, I don't have money or even a place to keep them," said Jasper, looking down at the books, a little ashamed of his ignorance.

Milo thought for a moment. "Tell ya how we'll handle it. You put them books back where you found them and we'll head home and talk to Mrs. Clemmens. We'll discuss your options about boarding and money. If we strike a deal, we'll come back and you can buy those books. How's that sound?"

"That sounds amicable, Mr. Clemmens," Jasper sheepishly answered and walked back to the bookshelves.

"What the heck is 'amicable'?" asked Alain.

"He agrees, Alain," said Milo under his breath.

After filling an extra gas can and stowing the pump, the two men went in to square up. Jasper was wandering around the store like it was a museum.

After a little more conversation, Milo called out, "Let's go, boy!" Jasper quickly walked to the men, extended his hand, and said, "It's been a pleasure meeting you, Mr. Alain Martin."

"Likewise, Jasper. I'm sure we'll meet again."

Jasper walked out to the tractor and positioned himself in front of the balancer. The two men chuckled.

Milo climbed aboard the 1911 Two-Speed Gear Drive International Harvester 12 Horsepower Type A Tractor, positioned the switches, and said, "Let her rip, Jasper!"

He gave it a spin, BOOM-CLACKER-CLACKER-BOOM, BOOM! came out of the tractor, and down the road they went.

CHAPTER IV
Gladys

Over an hour later, they pulled up to Milo's barn. The barn was big and red with a fresh coat of paint. The inviting smell of fresh hay filled the air.

"Have a look around, son, and I'll fetch Mrs. Clemmens." Both climbed down off the tractor. Milo headed to the farmhouse, confident that Gladys, his wife, would be happy with the company. They had lost their only daughter to consumption ten years before. Between their love and commitment to each other, and father time, their wounds were all but healed.

Jasper thought the home looked like a picture in a book! It had a big front yard with a white picket fence around it. A small chicken roost was on the side, between the house and the barn. Five hens and a rooster were pecking obsessively at the ground inside the fence. The home was a single-story prairie house with a big wraparound porch, a swing, and two rocking chairs near the front door.

Jasper turned around to look behind him. There were about three acres fenced in with barbed wire adjacent to the barn. An old milk cow and two mules were grazing. Towards the back a gray donkey was scratching his backside on a fence post. Later, he learned that farmers kept donkeys because they'd chase off coyotes and eat rattlesnakes. Jasper saw something move under a tuft of elm trees. Whatever it was had a set of four long legs. Jasper was baffled!

"Is that a camel?!" he blurted out.

"That's what it is, alright," answered Milo as he and Gladys walked up behind him.

"Like in The Arabian Nights?" Jasper was about to explode with excitement.

"Well, I guess so," stammered Milo. "Jasper, this is my wife, Mrs. Clemmens."

Jasper spun around and saw kind eyes, a captivating smile, and well-maintained, graying red hair. Her presence instantly comforted him.

"My pleasure, ma'am," Jasper said with a bow. He felt right at home with her.

"It's a pleasure to meet you too, Jasper." Smiling, she quietly took in the boy.

"Mr. Clemmens, why do you have a camel?" asked Jasper.

"Well, around ten years ago, he just turned up one morning. It seems the Army brought them out west as pack animals. They need a lot less food and water than mules. What the Army didn't know was how ornery they can be. They finally gave up on them and left them to the Comanches."

"Didn't the Comanches want them?" asked Jasper.

"Oh, they thought they were delicious! I guess this one got away and jumped our fence. A couple of braves would show up every now and then to wrangle him back. But he spit in their faces whenever they got too close to him. After a while I guess they just gave up. We've had him ever since."

"His name is Ali," said Mrs. Clemmens with a smile.

"Like The Arabian Nights," softly declared Jasper.

"Come in the house, and we'll get you settled in. I wish to know all about you, Mr. Jasper P. Whittington III," said Gladys, taking his arm.

"Settled in?" asked Jasper.

"That's right," chimed Milo. "We would like you to be our company until you figure out what you want to do. In the meantime, you can earn a little money helping me around the farm. How does that suit you?"

"Why, that suits me just fine, Mr. Clemmens." The kind offer touched his heart. Life had taken a turn for the better.

"Come with me," said Mrs. Clemmens.

Jasper was amazed and overwhelmed upon entering their home. It was so neat and clean. And oh! The wonderful aroma coming from the kitchen was intoxicating. There was an old piano in the corner and needlepoint doilies on every table. He remembered reading about a woman's touch in the Dickens novel Hard Times, and now understood.

Mrs. Clemmens continued, "Jasper, you're very welcome in our home, but at the moment, you're a bit ripe. Mr. Clemmens will take you to the barn and show you our wash tub. I'll fetch you some soap and a towel. I saved a pair of his old overalls. You can wear them until I get those clothes you're wearing clean."

Jasper's head was spinning. He had woken up this morning in a slowly deteriorating State Home where he had spent his entire life. This evening, he'd sit at the dinner table with the Clemmens family. Earlier, he'd had no idea how his day would end; now this. A warm place to sleep, good home cooking, and apparently, love. His mind was processing the vast shift. It was hard and it became difficult to speak. He didn't want to say anything to change the outcome of this adventure. And surely, this was the beginning of an adventure. Milo spoke to him on the way to the barn, but Jasper had no idea what he was saying. His mind just couldn't keep up.

Milo filled the wash tub with water and asked Jasper to join them in the house after he cleaned up. Jasper could only smile and nod. Mr. Clemmens left the barn. Jasper looked down at the soap and towel. He was too overwhelmed to speak.

Later he joined the couple for a visit in their parlor. Gladys had a million questions for him. "What happened to your family? Were you treated well? Did you leave any siblings?" etc., etc. He was a little overwhelmed by the barrage.

Milo remained silent during the talk, observing how Jasper handled himself under fire. He was impressed.

"Mama! My belly's rubbing my backbone! Let's eat!" demanded Milo.

"I hope you like pork stew and cornbread," said Gladys to Jasper.

"It smells like heaven, Mrs. Clemmens," said Jasper.

The three stood and headed to the kitchen table.

After the best dinner Jasper could recall, the trio sat at the dinner table and discussed options. What chores could Jasper do to earn his keep? How could he earn extra money? Where would he be in four years?

Jasper was touched by the generosity and kindness given by the couple. Between the gigantic 1911 Two-Speed Gear Drive International Harvester 12 Horsepower Type A Tractor and the camel, his mind grew weary and he had trouble keeping up with the conversation. Gladys noticed the boy waning.

"Let me show you where you'll sleep," she said, placing her hand on his shoulder.

"Yes, ma'am," was all he could muster up.

When the three stood, Milo stretched. That made Jasper smile, though Mrs. Clemmens seemed unimpressed with the display of poor table manners.

"Goodnight, Jasper," said Milo, walking out to the porch.

"Goodnight, Mr. Clemmens, and thank you for your generosity," he responded.

Gladys picked up an oil lamp sitting on the table. "Come this way, sugar."

The two followed the glowing light to the stairs at the end of the kitchen. His heart was already shoring up to Mrs. Clemmens. He truly wanted to belong here.

The day was taking its toll on him. He couldn't even think straight. Jasper followed Gladys up a small flight of stairs. Mrs. Clemmens opened the door at the top of the steps. It gently creaked open, and the soft, amber light spilled into the small room. There was a shipping trunk and an old iron trundle bed made with fresh linen and patch quilts. Set caddy-corner, next to the window was an oak washstand. A neatly folded towel was laid on the stand, along with a large white porcelain basin and a matching pitcher of water. And a toothbrush? His own toothbrush? He wouldn't have to share it?

"Is this all for me?" he asked sheepishly. Gladys took his hands into hers and smiled.

"Yes, it is, Jasper. Make yourself at home. Now you get yourself a good night's sleep. I'm sure tomorrow will be another big day. Goodnight, sugar," Gladys said as she turned to leave.

She left the lantern and closed the door behind her. He stood alone for a moment. Boy, he was knackered! The scent of lamp oil and fresh linen was luring him to bed. Jasper undressed and placed his neatly folded, newly acquired overalls on a small wooden chair by the door. He crawled into bed and wondered if there could be a more wonderful place in the world than right here. Surely not. Sleep took him quickly.

Jasper woke up to bright sunlight streaming through the single window in his room. He got up, washed, got dressed, and headed downstairs. The smell was incredible and very familiar.

"What's that smell?!" he blurted. Catching himself, he said, "Excuse me, Mrs. Clemmens. I mean, good morning." Gladys smiled and responded, "Good morning, Jasper! That's bacon and eggs. Grab a seat at the table and pour yourself some milk."

"Where's Mr. Clemmens?" he asked as he filled his glass.

"Oh, he's had his breakfast. He's in the barn, tending the animals. We're normally up by five every morning," she said as she cracked an egg into the frying pan.

"What time is it now?" asked Jasper.

Gladys looked down at her watch broach and said, "Well, it's coming up on eight o'clock."

"Tarnation! I've slept half the morning away!" Jasper exclaimed as he rose from the table.

"Now you sit down and eat your breakfast!" demanded Gladys. "We wanted you to sleep in. You had a pretty big day yesterday. You can start your chores after you eat."

After very quick consideration, he agreed and sat back down. Man! That bacon smelled good.

"Help yourself to some biscuits and jelly. Your eggs will be done lickity-split."

The biscuits were still warm and very fluffy. With a generous helping of homemade butter and grape jelly, the biscuits alone made a good breakfast. Mrs. Clemmens put a plate in front of him with two strips of bacon, two fried eggs, and slices of tomato.

"Here you are, sugar," she said.

He looked at the plate with the same admiration one would give a Christmas goose.

"Well, dig in!" encouraged Gladys, shaking him from a long stare. He dug! No more than 90 seconds later, Jasper mopped his plate clean with a fresh biscuit. The sight made Mrs. Clemmens smile.

Jasper rose from the table and wiped his chin.

"Is there anything I can do for you before I head out, ma'am?" Gladys only smiled and pointed to her cheek. Jasper walked over, kissed her on the cheek, and bolted out the door. Gladys giggled and wiped off a little egg yoke. She was aglow the rest of the morning.

And so, Jasper P. Whittington's life began a new chapter. On his first day on the farm, Jasper and Milo walked the majority of the forty acres to help Jasper get acquainted with his new home. They walked to the property behind the house. There was a twenty-acre field of cleared flatland were Milo rotated crops of corn, peanuts, and onions.

Behind the field was a small patch of scrub oak and a pigpen. There were no hogs now, but Milo would soon pick up three fresh-weaned piglets to raise for butcher. A creek, which almost always had water, ran behind the pigsty, and a small ditch channeled water from the creek to the pen.

"Pigs need to waller in mud to keep off the parasites," explained Milo.

Towards the west property line were a few giant cottonwoods. They must have been at least a hundred feet high. Among the big trees was a fairytale gazebo. Worn and tattered now, it seemed to have lived past its prime. Jasper then realized who it was for. Mrs. Clemmens had spoken only a little about Tessa. You could tell she was still dealing with the loss of her daughter.

After a tour of the Clemmens farm, Jasper could now see his new life. This was where he belonged, and these were the people he should be around.

Monthly chores were added to his weekly chores, and weekly chores were added to his daily ones. He learned to use the 1911 Two-Speed Gear Drive International Harvester 12 Horsepower Type A Tractor for chores on the farm and trips into town. Contentment, happiness, and lots of love filled his day-to-day life. He looked forward to the holidays now. The town of Pryor had festivals and parades to celebrate all occasions. Christmas and Thanksgiving were amazing. The 4th of July was extra special as it was also the day Gladys selected to celebrate Jasper's birthday, which hadn't been a consideration at the State Home. Any time Gladys wanted to go to town for a parade, Jasper would fetch the milk stool and assist her in climbing onto the tractor. That in itself was fun to watch.

Jasper not only mastered riding the donkey, but he also became quite a celebrity by riding the camel into town! He would tie him off at the watering trough in front of Mr. Martin's store. Everyone in town would stop by to see Ali. All the kids loved him, and Mr. Martin didn't mind the traffic.

Jasper's desire to learn hadn't faded. As he began earning money, he ordered new books from Mr. Martin. Jasper would go through his vendor catalogs to pick out the titles he wanted. He loved the modern age and wanted to read about new technology. The title that stood out the most was Alfred Lawson's "Aircraft," an introduction to the nuts and bolts of powered flight. Jasper dreamed of someday building and flying his own airplane.

After Jasper had been living with the Clemmens for three years, Gladys's health took a turn for the worse. The doctor said she had cardiovascular disease. She was weak and a little distant, but her eyes always lit up when she saw Milo and Jasper. She was aware of her poor health but remained happy and full of love. Jasper and Milo now prepared most of the meals and cleaned up.

On the next 4th of July, Gladys was too weak to make it to the parade so they stayed home. Instead, she sat at the kitchen table and coached the men on preparing a peach cobbler and homemade vanilla ice cream. The cobbler came out looking a bit abstract, but it was still delicious. They then sat on the porch, enjoying the treat, while they watched the fireworks being shot off near town.

"Jasper," said Gladys.

"Yes, ma'am," said Jasper.

"Come over here and sit next to me so I don't have to holler at you," she said, smiling.

Jasper walked over and sat next to her. Gladys reached out and took his hand.

"Every day you've been with us has been a blessing," she said.

"That's right!" chimed in Milo.

"I can tell that the Lord is calling me, sugar." Jasper's eyes clouded from her words.

"But you still got a while, Mrs. Clemmens. Right?" said Jasper.

"Oh, I don't know, baby. It could be ten years, it could be tomorrow. For the last few months, I've been thinking we're all part of a long, unfinished story and my chapter is ending. Baby, I was an orphan, just like you, living with some kin when I met Milo. I was sixteen and he was at the ripe old age of nineteen. And look at us now. We shared lots of laughs and lots of tears. And Milo still looks at me the same way. He even steals a kiss now and then. I love him more now than ever. Watching you grow into a fine young man, packed full of dreams, has been my best medicine. You made me feel like a mother again," Gladys said as she fiddled with her watch, something she did when deep in thought.

Milo sat listening quietly. The only sound he made was a gentle clink as he emptied his ice cream bowl.

Gladys continued, "You and Milo have helped me come to terms with the loss of Tessa. I'm happy now, and soon I'll see her again. You know, I thought I'd die with a broken heart, but I was wrong. Jasper, this is as happy as I have ever been." Gladys paused and looked directly into Jasper's eyes and said, "Now you go out and find your own happiness."

"I'm happy here, Mrs. Clemmens. I don't want to go anywhere. This is my family. This is my home. This is where I belong," said Jasper, not wanting to face the harsh reality that they would soon lose her.

Gladys squeezed his hand and said, "Now listen! You need to find yourself a good woman and raise you a family. Milo found you standing on the side of the road without a plan. That doesn't sound to me like the end of a story but the beginning. There are plenty more chapters coming, son. You make sure you turn every page and read every word. And find someone you can share your story with. Find your home."

"This is my home, Mrs. Clemmens," Jasper repeated, his tone softer and sadder.

They sat quietly until Ali bellowed as another firework exploded into a mass of green and red sparkles that slowly faded as they fell.

"No, honey, this here is your journey. Me, Mr. Clemmens, and even Ali, are just part of your journey. Your home is still waiting and you got a long way to go. You'll need to take the hard times with the good because sometimes hard times guide you better than good ones. And keep your heart open, or when you see home you might miss it."

"Jasper, you're growing into a fine young man. This here world needs people like you. People like you make it a better place. Go and find your home and start your family," she said.

She gazed over at Milo and smiled. Milo simply nodded, his face softening under the weight of her words.

CHAPTER V
Richard Elliott Standish, Esq.

April 2nd, 1915

Now, at eighteen, Jasper sat alone, lost in thought, in an Elizabethan chair in front of a mahogany desk. Leather-bound books with gold-leaf titles surrounded him. He did not recognize the books, but he did recognize the smell of old cigars and whiskey. He was sitting in the office of Richard Elliott Standish, Esq., the family lawyer for the Clemmens estate.

Today, he and Jasper were finalizing the transfer of the farm. Milo had made it clear in his will that Jasper would inherit all properties and liquid assets. Before Milo, Jasper never had two nickels to rub together. Now this! After a discussion in the next room, Mr. Standish returned to the office with two secretaries and a notary public. Legal talk and scores of signings ensued.

Small talk finished the meeting, and the three departed, leaving Jasper and the lawyer alone.

"This must be a lot to take in, Mr. Whittington. Go home and organize your thoughts. Your decisions can carry unanticipated consequences now that you're a man of means. I'm afraid your childhood is over." Mr. Standish gently placed a hand on Jasper's shoulder. "Come back and see me on the 9th. We'll start hammering out a plan for you. Don't worry, son. It will all work out."

Only two weeks earlier, he had woken in the usual manner and gone to the kitchen for coffee and breakfast. No one was there, so the house felt unsettled. It was as if something was missing, something was wrong. He walked to the barn to be greeted by a hungry lot. None of the animals had been fed, and the cow needed milking.

"Mr. Clemmens?" called Jasper. There was no answer, so Jasper fed the livestock, milked Junebug, and returned to the house. Entering the still-silent home, he called again, "Mr. Clemmens?" There was no answer. He walked to their bedroom and found Milo sitting on the bed. Gladys lay quietly; Milo was holding her hand.

"She's gone," said Milo meekly. Jasper felt a cold, painful jolt. The fact that she was dying never seemed real to him. Her smile and kind words always calmed him and made him believe everything would be alright.

Milo always seemed at home sitting anywhere. Now, sitting next to Mrs. Clemmens, he was a broken-hearted man, slouched, his eyes with no sparkle. His spirit was leaving him. Without diverting his blank stare, Milo said, "Jasper, could you go into town and fetch Dr. Cagle and the preacher?" His monotone voice trailed off.

"Yes, sir," muttered Jasper, trying to hold back his emotions.

Jasper climbed onto the tractor, set the switches, stepped back down, and spun the balancer. BOOM, CLACKER, CLACKER, BOOM! BOOM!

Within an hour, Jasper had stopped in front of Dr. Cagle's practice. He explained what had happened and asked if the doctor could come and bring the Reverend. Dr. Cagle drove his 1915 Oldsmobile Model 42 to the rector to pick up Reverend Bill Williams. Soon, they were passing Jasper on the road to the farm. Jasper arrived twenty minutes later and found the two men waiting on the porch.

"Jasper, why didn't you say anything about Milo?" asked Dr. Cagle.

Jasper curiously asked, "What?" Then panic rushed over him. He ran into the house and to the bedroom. Milo was lying on the bed next to Gladys. It was as if they were asleep. It was too much for Jasper. His heart leapt out of his chest. He knelt silently on the floor for fear of fainting. Life had taken a turn for the worse.

April 9th, 1915

"Are you sure about this?" asked Counselor Standish.

"I've thought about it long and hard, Mr. Standish. I have planned to do it for years – the traveling bit, anyway. And I think it would make Mr. and Mrs. Clemmens proud," answered Jasper.

The lawyer was amazed at how much more Jasper sounded like a man, as though he had let go of his boyish ways.

During the week between their meetings, Jasper had devised a plan that surprised Mr. Standish. The farm was to be converted into a home for unwed mothers. A full-time staff would provide medical, educational, and vocational assistance. When possible, the patients would help with the chores (Ali and Junebug would always have a home) and a $25,000 trust fund would serve to finance the home. Mr. Standish would manage funding, investments, and taxes.

As for Jasper, he would accept a one-time payment of five hundred dollars. His personal plan was to go to Norman, Oklahoma, to continue his educational pursuits at Oklahoma University.

"Well, Pryor will always remember you, Jasper. You have made us a better community," said Mr. Standish.

"Thank you," Jasper responded. "Your help has made it all possible, and I truly believe Mrs. Clemmens is guiding me."

"When do you plan to head out?" asked the counselor.

"I'll leave in the morning. I can take my entrance exam at any time, but I won't be able to enroll until the Fall. I'll find a job nearby to keep me until then."

"What do you plan on studying?" asked Standish.

"When I was younger, I wanted to be a doctor. Now, I'm sure it will be something in literature," said Jasper.

"That makes sense, son. Best of luck!" Standish extended his hand to Jasper, who shook it and thanked the counselor again.

Early the next morning Jasper rode Ali to Martin's General Store, holding his one and only bag in hand. Mr. Martin had assured Jasper he would get Ali back home.

Jasper was a bundle of nerves, though he was excited about the new adventure. In his short life, he had discovered that the unknown parts of his future could be the most rewarding, but he was also aware that the worst could be yet to come. Life was bound to take a new road in the most unanticipated directions at the most unexpected times.

He was a young man now. Ready for new adventures. The loss of Mr. and Mrs. Clemmens still left a big hole in his heart. But the new charity had become a reality, and the home for unwed mothers existed because of their passing.

Friends, acquaintances, and even people he didn't know lined the railroad platform to say goodbye to Jasper. His presence had been a welcome and interesting change in Pryor, Oklahoma's mundane, day-to-day life. As he boarded the 2:18 to Oklahoma City, he began to feel doubts about leaving. He was sure he would never feel as appreciated as he did in Pryor. But life was calling. He would get an education, pursue his adventures, and make his fortune. Then, he would return to settle down here, form a household, and tell his stories.

With a loud hiss of steam, the train lurched forward. Jasper looked out at the familiar faces as the people of Prior waved and cheered. The whistle blew as the train slowly left the station. This was to be the last time he'd see Pryor, Oklahoma.

CHAPTER VI
The Calling

April 19th, 1915

Jasper stepped out of the Oklahoma University Administration Building. He was walking on air! Not only was his application accepted, but he had been granted a scholarship in Literature! He wouldn't even need to pay for his food if he maintained his grades. This was a dream come true. He would now earn a degree from a major university.

Walking back to his hotel, Jasper had an idea. He should celebrate.

He abstained from drink, but he wanted to do something. Walking past the Liberty Theatre, he was inspired. The marquee read "Civilization" and "News Reels." Daily matinees only cost a nickel, and he had earned it. Jasper approached the kiosk and asked the gentleman operator when the show would start.

"Ten minutes or so," he answered casually.

Jasper laid down the nickel and got his ticket. He hadn't been to many picture shows, they were just a novelty to him. He was more interested in the war in Europe. Major technological breakthroughs were showing up on the battlefield, and this, indeed, interested him, especially combat airplanes. He had seen a few of them circling over Tinker Airfield. The sound of the powerful engines enthralled him. He already had a strong understanding of basic aeronautics, but the powerplants were something he needed to get his hands on to better understand.

He entered the smoke-filled theatre, which seated fifty people, but there were no more than ten today. A bare bulb shined brightly in the back of the quiet room. A sharp click came from the projection booth as the one light was extinguished. A fluttering mechanical sound came from the projector and the small pump organ wheezed as the operator started the film.

"News of the Day!" lit up the screen. "The Hun have taken Belgium and executed entire villages." Next, a tombstone of a newborn infant in French read, "Pierre Montclair, Born March 3rd, 1915, and Died March 3rd, 1915. Shot to death by Germans." As the English translations appeared on screen, gasps came from the audience. "Our brave allies are battling the Hun from the ground and the air!" In the next scene French soldiers climbed out of a muddy trench. Then, oh my! The airplanes! What magnificent technology! What incredible bravery!

Jasper had an out-of-body experience. He could feel the cold wind on his face, the airframe vibrations and the tug of the yoke. He could hear the roar of the powerful engine and the crack of the synchronized guns, and smelled the petrol, exhaust, and gunpowder. War was calling Jasper. Could it be that his entire life has led him to this point? "This is my calling, my adventure," he declared.

Though he stayed for the feature, Jasper couldn't remember a thing about the movie. He had been lost in thought. How could he become a part of this new age? America had no intention of entering the war. To become a true aviator, he'd need to make it to France and volunteer for the Lafayette Flying Corps. But what about the university? The scholarship? It must be put on hold. He felt duty calling. By the end of the main feature, Jasper had decided to leave for New York City and book a passage to Europe that week.

April 20th, 1915

"And you're sure this is your final decision, Mr. Whittington?" asked Professor Sullivan.

"As sure as the sun will rise, professor," answered Jasper. "I've thought long and hard about it."

The professor continued, encouraging the boy to think again. "But it was just yesterday you accepted the scholarship. What has changed your mind?"

"The call of duty. I truly feel I can make a difference in the war," Jasper said with some reverence.

"I appreciate the valor of a man answering 'the call,' son, but you must understand that every day, coffins are filled by this calling. All of us on this staff believe you have a good future with the university. Won't you please reconsider?"

Jasper responded, "I can't thank you enough for the opportunity to be a part of this great institution, but . . ."

"The call of duty," the professor finished his sentence. "It's a story as old as time, young Whittington. You'll be in our prayers," he said, extending his hand. "Come back after you have slain your dragons, Mr. Whittington. Surely, we'll have room for you."

"Thank you, professor. I shall," answered Jasper.

After shaking his hand, Jasper left the room and quietly closed the door. Professor Sullivan sat behind his desk, pulled out a flask and tumbler, and poured a little whiskey. From a cigar box on his desktop, he removed what would eventually be called a "Churchill" and trimmed the end. Then he gently dipped the trimmed end in the whiskey. He struck a match and carefully lit it without touching it with the fire. He drew deeply, then let out a slow exhale. The professor felt like he'd seen a unicorn with no others to witness. That was the smartest kid, with more potential than he'd seen in years, and he'd never see him again.

CHAPTER VII
New York City

April 29th, 1915

The train pulled into Grand Central Station and shook to a stop. Jasper deboarded and looked up at the giant four-faced clock above him, which read 5:00 p.m. Jasper was overwhelmed by the sheer number of people on the platform in New York City. He'd never been in such a large crowd, and he'd never had strangers bump into him without even an "Excuse me!"

Jasper saw a sign above a breezeway that said, "Ocean Passage." Following the corridor, he emerged into the Grand Central lobby. There was a kiosk with the sign "Lusitania to Liverpool." At the window was a man wearing a white shirt, a bow tie, and a transparent green visor. His huge handlebar mustache must have been a point of pride for the gentleman, as it was extensively groomed.

"Good evening, sir." Jasper naturally greeted people with respect and a smile. "I seek passage to Liverpool." The man responded with a snarky smile and nod, and said, "You're a bit late, son. The only remaining tickets are first class. Lucy departs on Saturday. She'll be the last departure this spring. The next passage is in July."

"Who's Lucy?" asked Jasper.

The man rolled his eyes and answered, "The Lusitania, she's scheduled for a departure at 1:30 p.m." His tone made it abundantly clear he was looking to end this transaction.

Still cordial, Jasper asked, "How much is first class?"

Without looking up from his desk, the man barked, "One hundred forty-two dollars and seventy cents."

The price stunned Jasper. He had never seen a transaction over five dollars! And now, forty-two dollars! But he had to get to France, and he had the money. Still smiling, begrudgingly, he reached into his vest pocket, pulled out two twenties and a five, and placed the cash before the rude man.

The mustachioed man looked at the money and, without looking up, repeated, "ONE HUNDRED and forty-two dollars and seventy cents."

Jasper felt a jolt through his entire body and thought, "So this is what it's like to have a heart attack!"

Silently, he spun around, reached into his secret pocket and pulled out one of his hundred-dollar bills. His desire to get to France drove him as he passed it to the clerk with great pain and trepidation, along with his newly minted passport.

After seeing the hundred-dollar bill, the clerk's attention fixed on the young man's face. He was too poorly dressed and too young to have this much money. But now, for whatever reason, it appeared he was dealing with a young man of considerable means.

The clerk's demeanor completely flipped. "Shall I send for your luggage, sir? We have begun loading."

"No, thank you. This is my only luggage," Jasper said, lifting a carpet bag.

A flash of suspicion swept over the man. Could the boy be a desperate criminal on the run? Should he contact an authority? It was probably safer not to get involved. He could be a dangerous man. Whatever the case, the quicker they finished their transaction, the safer he would feel. The clerk added Jasper to the ship's registry and handed him his ticket and passport.

"Much obliged!" said Jasper, still reeling from the astronomical ticket price.

"Of course, sir! If there's nothing else, we shall see you at boarding on Saturday, May 1st, at 1:00 p.m., Dock 54."

May 1st, 1915

Jasper P. Whittington had breathed different air for the last two days. Walking the streets of Manhattan and Brooklyn fascinated him. Food vendors were on every street, and huge markets sold everything from fresh carrots to live monkeys.

A janitor at the YMCA had warned him that New York pickpockets would "clean him out" if he didn't button every pocket and stay clear of crowds. The janitor was the first black man Jasper had ever conversed with. Actually, he was the first black man he'd ever seen. He had read novels describing life shared with the black community, but this was his first experience. In Pryor, nothing good was said about black folks, but most of the people there had never been outside of Pryor's city limits.

After spending a few days conversing with Lester Picket, a first-generation immigrant from the Jamaican Isle, Jasper now knew better. At first, it was challenging to understand the man. But after a few encounters, Jasper picked up on his rhythm and banter and enjoyed his speech. Lester was a good soul and an intelligent man. Jasper was glad to make his acquaintance. Lester was shocked when Jasper extended his hand to bid farewell, but he shook it just the same. The meeting had been a good experience for both of them.

Now, with ticket and bag in hand, he was standing on the deck of the Lusitania. The ocean breeze swept away the city rot. He marveled at the sheer size of the ship. He knew to say ship instead of boat from reading Treasure Island. Watching the deckhands follow the first mate's orders and the tugboats maneuver the massive ship was like watching a ballet. He could have easily seen himself as a world-traveling deckhand, but he had a plan for now. To fly airplanes.

"Shall I see you to your cabin, sir?" asked the black porter.

"Of course," answered Jasper with a tip of his hat. The gesture initially took the porter back. You could tell he wasn't accustomed to friendly replies from passengers. It put a little skip in his step. The porter led Jasper to Cabin 104 and opened the door to a beautiful, storybook-like room. With a flick of a switch, the miracle of electricity lighted up the room – cutting-edge technology!

"Will there be anything else, sir?" asked the porter. Jasper turned to him, pulled out a one-dollar bill, and held it up.

"What's your name, mister?" asked Jasper, making deliberate eye contact.

The question sent shivers down the porter's spine. He recapped the encounter and could not see anything that would have attracted the gentleman's ire.

He stiffened his stance and answered, "John Adams Smitherman, sir."

Jasper responded, "John Adams Smitherman, I need you to keep a close eye on me. You see, this is not my world. I'm as nervous as a cat with a long tail in a room full of rocking chairs. If you see a time during this voyage when I may get my tail rocked on, could I count on your experience to safely guide me?"

"I'm at your service . . . mister?" Smitherman paused.

"Jasper P. Whittington III," answered Jasper.

"I'm at your service, Mr. Whittington," said the porter, easing his stance.

"Thank you," said Jasper.

The porter genuinely smiled and left the room.
And land sakes! What a room!

CHAPTER VIII
The Journey

May 7th, 1915

After three days of rough seas and rainy weather, Liverpool was almost in sight. The seven-day journey was nearly over. The mighty ship seemed to have a knack for calming an angry ocean. She hardly tossed at all from the storms.

Jasper's "inside man," John Adams Smitherman, had kept him abreast of all the ship's gossip about the strange man with no luggage and no lady to accompany him. Maybe he was an arms dealer or German spy. Or perhaps a trained assassin on a secret passage to Europe to end the war by taking out a head of state.

Let them talk. Jasper shared his plans with John and no one else. He felt too much like a country bumpkin to interact with the first-class passengers and thought it would draw too much attention if he socialized with the others. At least, that was advice from the good porter. John woke him this morning with breakfast. He had been taking all his meals in his room. He even politely passed on a dinner invitation from the captain. John said it had raised his dander a bit!

It was May 7th. They should be docking just before supper. The news invigorated Jasper. The longest leg of the trip was almost over. Soon, he would be crossing the English countryside on a train. He had yet to see the train departures from Liverpool but after surveying a map, Dover seemed to be his next logical destination.

Jasper finished his meal and cleaned up. Wanting to walk off his breakfast, he put on his only suit and stepped out on deck. What a perfect morning! The sun was out in full glory. The sweet and inviting aroma of the clean ocean air filled his lungs. This was exactly where he should be.

The upper deck was truly marvelous. Several first-class passengers strolled around the deck with their little dogs as Jasper leaned over the rail, watching children playing on a lower deck. What a great adventure this must be for them. What stories they would tell.

While looking down, Jasper saw John the porter walking with a case of wine. He wanted to greet him, but it would have been in poor taste. Besides, John's hands were full. Jasper quietly watched him maneuver the case around the screaming and laughing kids. A little girl stumbled during an impromptu dance, fell, and began to cry. John stopped, set down the wine, and attended to the child.

A survivor described what happened next: "It sounded like a million-ton hammer hitting a steam boiler a hundred feet high."

As Jasper watched John Adams Smitherman attend to the young girl, they vanished in a dark cloud of black smoke and fire. In an instant, the air was filled with shards of splintered deck and red-hot metal shrapnel. All accompanied by a thunderous roar.

Jasper found himself several feet in the air above the deck. He came back down hard enough to momentarily knock him out. Though the explosion muffled his hearing, he still heard people screaming for help. He managed to get to his knees and tried to stand. Then he felt the upper deck flex, rocked by another explosion.

This explosion threw him over the deck railing, which he managed to grab to stop his fall. Jasper looked down and saw a cavernous hole on Lucy's starboard side. Dark black smoke and bright orange flames poured from the hole. He saw people on fire jumping from the flames into the water.

"This is not how I'm going to die!" Jasper shouted.

He pulled himself back over the railing as the ship began to list. The reality of what happened washed over him. They'd been attacked.

Such was the nature of war. The faces of the dead and dying were not that of valiant heroes. They were just people. The cries were not what he expected to hear in battle. They were from women and children. Every soul on the ship had been changed forever. Jasper felt camaraderie with the survivors around him, all strangers just moments before.

"Lifeboats! We need to get to the lifeboats," thought Jasper.

He looked down to see three sinking lifeboats near the gaping hole. They were shredded. Further toward the bow other boats were being positioned for boarding. The wide-eyed crew members were panicking. Clearly, they didn't know what they were doing. No instructions had been given to them and there had been no practice drills.

Several passengers attempting to board the lifeboats lost their footing and fell over 40 feet into the water. Jasper saw a woman with a child in her arms fall against the ship's hull and bounce lifelessly into the water. The sight stunned him, so he looked away.

"To the lifeboats! Abandon ship!" shouted the first mate from the bulwark.

Jasper ran across the deck to board a nearby lifeboat, but then saw the ship's list had become so severe that the boats laid uselessly against the hull. He was alone on the deck. Everyone else had run to Lucy's other side to try the lifeboats there. As he made his way to join them, he saw other passengers jumping into the oily, polluted water. He watched in horror as a lifeboat broke loose and landed on top of another, certainly killing at least thirty people; jumping seemed like the best of all bad options. He looked down to see the vile water catch fire and set alight some twenty-five other passengers and crew.

Only half the ship was still above water. Standing on the sloping upper deck, he was only ten feet above the water now. Surely, jumping was his last and only option. Which was fearful if one didn't know how to swim. Just below him was a mass of debris. A large piece of the lower deck floated nearby. He'd be OK if he could just reach it.

Feeling the ship being drawn down, Jasper knew he must jump, NOW. He held on tightly with both hands and carefully stepped over the railing. The sounds of cracking wood and twisting steel assaulted his ears. Great hisses of air were being forced out of the ship, which covered the passengers' screams. He jumped.

Jasper hit the water within arm's reach of the deck piece. He felt his foot hit another passenger's head below the water. A feeling of guilt rushed over him as he clung to the piece of deck and rested his head on the boards. As he floated, he noticed the piece had been painted for shuffleboard. "Hmm . . ." he said aloud.

He snapped out of it when the sinking ship began drawing him down. He lifted himself out of the water onto the floating deck, stabilized himself, and reached back to retrieve the person he had landed on, but no one was there. Instead, Jasper saw a piece of debris that could make a good paddle, managed to grab it, and paddled away.

He was going to make it! He sensed some relief from that thought, but physical pain brought him back to the moment. The side of his ribcage throbbed. As he pulled away from the sinking ship, the sound of escaping air and shattering glass grew distant.

Suddenly, the raft bumped to a stop. Jasper turned to see a young woman trying to pull herself onto the piece of shuffleboard deck, but her waterlogged dress made it difficult. Her head and face were severely burned. She had no hair left and one eye swollen shut. Jasper reached over to pull her up, but the skin on her forearm let go when he tried. The dark ocean swallowed her.

Eighteen minutes after the attack, the Lusitania slipped under the bubbling, burning water. Now, cries of the people, in shock and agony, were accompanied only by the sound of soft waves and seagulls. Jasper lifted his head and looked beyond his makeshift raft to see three lifeboats floating in the dingy water. A few passengers were clinging to debris, and many more were floating face down, called by the Lord, he was certain. He wanted to help the others but was in so much pain he dared not move.

His left ear was deaf. He reached to touch the ear and found that the side of his face was covered in blood. He moved his hand to check for more injuries, but it caused too much pain, so he stopped. He remembered seeing the coast of Ireland just before the attack. "We should be rescued soon," he thought as he rolled onto his back and closed his eyes.

CHAPTER IX
The Good Father

May 10th, 1915

Jasper was sitting alone on the front porch at the farm in Pryor when Milo stepped out and handed him one of the two cups of coffee he was carrying. They greeted each other with a smile and a nod.

The aroma of fresh-cut wheat filled the cool morning air as Jasper looked out over the farm. The two mules, and Junebug and Ali stood grazing near the barn. A serene feeling of contentment washed over him as if he had accomplished something great. He looked back at Milo, who didn't return his gaze.

"Milo?" inquired Jasper, but he did not respond. "Mr. Clemmens, everything alright, sir?"

There was still no reply as Milo stared blankly at the pasture. Then he slowly turned and made direct eye contact. A tear rolled down his left cheek as he did, but the blank stare remained. Milo moaned as if in pain, but his lips remained closed. Panic began to show in his eyes. He trembled violently but still didn't open his mouth. His moans grew louder. Jasper reached over to touch his arm and quickly drew back. The skin was scalding hot. Milo suddenly burst into flames. Stunned, Jasper looked up and saw the porch and the entire home in flames. Milo then let out a gut-wrenching scream.

Jasper jolted awake. He was in a tiny room in someone else's home. There were photos on the washstand he did not recognize. The room was quaint but very different. Even the linen was distinct. Was he in a nightshirt? He never wore a nightshirt! He didn't remember going to bed or even undressing. How did I get here? Wasn't I on the Lusitania?

Visions of the violent attack rushed back. Where was John Adams Smitherman? His heart sank when he remembered. John, the little girl he was helping, and all the children on the deck were gone – no more.

The bedroom door opened and an old man came in carrying what would be Jasper's first meal in days. He was dressed like a holy man. "A Catholic priest?" Jasper thought. A thin, pale, bald man wearing a brown tweed suit and a stiff smile followed the priest in.

"I thought you were stirring about!" said the old priest.

"Where am I?" Jasper asked as he managed to sit up, his rough and stiff voice stuck in his throat from days of silence.

"You're in Cobh," responded the priest.

"Where's Cobh?" asked Jasper.

"You're on the south coast of Ireland. I'm Father William Wallace Hoy. This is my home," he said.

The other man interrupted impatiently, "Yes, and I'm Walter Page, U.S. Ambassador to Great Britain.

I've been in town for a few days now. It's good to see you looking well. I'm here to. . ."

Father Hoy stopped him and said, "Tell me what you remember, son."

"I remember seeing the coast of Ireland from the upper deck," said Jasper, in a neutral tone, looking out the window. His eyes narrowed as he strained to organize his thoughts. "I saw John Smitherman disappear in a cloud of fire and black smoke. . . with a small girl." Jasper's lips tightened. Speaking became difficult. Twice he opened his mouth and nothing came out. He had to force speech. "A woman was trying to climb out of the water. She was badly burned. Her skin. . . it was hanging off. I took her arm, but her flesh slid, and she slipped into the water." Jasper began shaking uncontrollably. He began to cry. "A woman, holding a baby, fell against the ship's hull . . ." Jasper's face fell into his hands. Sobs were all he could manage.

"It was a horrible accident, my son. Just . . ." began the priest

Jasper cut off the priest and cried. "It was no accident! It was an intentional attack! The people who did this are murderers!" Jasper had his voice back. "This was a wanton act of violence by some godless Germans." He fell silent again, lay on his back, and stared at the ceiling. The ambassador was stunned to silence by Jasper's outburst.

Father Hoy had read in "The General Advisor" about the attack on the Lusitania and the German apology. Since then, the Father had been praying for the strength to forgive. Looking at this young, broken man, he thought he might leave the forgiving up to the Lord. He stood, placed his hand on Jasper's shoulder, and said, "They truly have earned the wrath of God." Father Hoy walked to the door, turned, and said, "You need your rest, my boy."

"But I . . ." came from the ambassador's mouth. Father Hoy silenced him and led him out of the room to leave Jasper alone.

"Eat and rest, my son," advised the Father.

Ambassador Page stopped once the door was closed and said, "Father, I need to talk to this boy. We still need to contact his family. The ship's registry confirmation is past due, and my report on the survivors is also past due."

The priest nodded but said firmly, "Before you get any information from him, he'll need to adjust to his surroundings. He's overwhelmed, confused, and in pain just now. Let's try it again in the morning."

The ambassador was flustered. "Father, I have been away from my post for too long now. I'll be back here this afternoon."

"There's no use for that, good sir. I am now the boy's advocate. I assure you he will be undisturbed for the rest of the day." The Father politely added, "Allow me to show you to the door."

The ambassador's stiff smile changed to a mild grimace. "Morning indeed," he mumbled.

May 12th, 1915

Jasper was eleven years old sitting in his favorite chair at The Whitaker Home. Candles, holly, and mistletoe adorned the grand room. He read aloud "A Christmas Carol" for several younger children on the floor, as they gazed up at him in fascination. The warmth and aroma of the Christmas Eve fire set the mood for the cautionary tale – don't allow life to steal away your holiday spirit. The kids seemed dazed as they absorbed the poetic story.

In an instant, their faces lost all expression. Their heads turned slowly toward the hearth. The light reflected in the children's eyes as the fire quickly grew. It roared louder and the room became unbearably hot. The ear-splitting sound of an ocean liner's horn bellowed. Pictures, glasses, and furniture rattled violently.

Flames now leapt from the hearth. The children turned to face the ever-growing fire. Jasper looked on with horror as, one-by-one, each child stood, ambled towards the fierce fire, and slowly walked into the flame. Their hair instantly burned away, and their skin charred and bubbled. No child cried, but he could see the pain in their eyes. The last in line was a small girl. She turned and walked back to Jasper, and with a blank stare said, "Come with us, Jasper. It's your calling."

Jasper forced himself awake. He was terrified but now knew it was just a dream. This was his fifth night in Ireland; a nightmare had accompanied all five.

Three days after the attack, an orderly from the hospital brought him his one and only suit. He checked the secret pocket in the vest and, lo and behold, he found three one-dollar and three hundred-dollar bills.

Finally, a stroke of good luck had secured his passage home. Going back to Oklahoma was now his only desire. The horror and pain of war had made themselves clear. He had been an orphan his whole life but never felt more hopeless than he did right now. The glory of war was a myth. He now knew he was a man of peace.

Interviews with Ambassador Page were difficult. Jasper was in physical pain and still in shock over witnessing the enormous loss of life, but he understood the ambassador needed to complete his duties. His bedside manner could have used some polishing. His queries were cold and distant. Maybe it was the ambassador's way of processing the tragedy, but Jasper doubted it. He just wasn't a very nice man.

Jasper was always a bundle of nerves after Ambassador Page left. Father Hoy would give him the only medicine he knew would calm him – a shot of whiskey. Jasper had never touched the bottle before, but when he took a shot, it warmed his insides and steadied his nerves. He quickly developed a taste for it.

Still stiff from the shipwreck, he worked himself out of bed slowly. After washing up and brushing his teeth with his finger, he made his way to the kitchen table. Father Hoy was there enjoying a cup of tea and a good read.

The Father greeted him brightly, "Good morning, Mr. Whittington. Did you get some rest?"

"I did, Father. Thank you." Jasper made a cup of tea. "Tea, Father?"

"No, thank you, Jasper. I just made one. When are you boarding?" asked the Father.

"If I'm on the docks by noon, I'll be fine," said Jasper as he sat down. "Father, your generosity has surely put me on the path to recovery. I'll never be able to repay you."

"Hush, my son. You are a gift from God, my penance, a chance to be a good Christian, and I've enjoyed keeping the ambassador at arm's length. Squeezing his deep pocketbook for your ticket back to America was also very fulfilling," the priest said triumphantly. He then added, "Do you have money for travel?"

"I do, Father." Jasper paused and stared into his cup of tea, "Father, I'm afraid to get on another ship."

"Tsk, my son! Not only has God made a clear statement that he has a plan for you, but no U-boat has been spotted since the attack on the Lusitania. And I believe your fellow countrymen have sent a stern message by deploying their navy to the British Isles."

"It's not so much the U-boats. It's being in the company of others who can't know how I feel." Much of Jasper's buoyant personality had disappeared, and he was afraid he'd never feel normal again.

"Sometimes you need to take the problem by the tail and look it square in the eye!" said Father Hoy.

"Indeed, Father," Jasper replied with a forced smile.

At noon, the two men stood on the dock, staring up at the massive RMS Adriatic, considered the largest ship in the world and truly a wonder to a boy from Oklahoma. The loading of the luggage and goods was complete. Jasper was noticeably shaken – not by the ship but by the people boarding.

"Now, son. Find your nerve. You're still the man you were before the attack. Faith, strength, and fortitude are still inside you, lad. Spend this voyage reestablishing yourself."

"I'm so nervous, Father. All those people, they'll think I'm a loon." Father Hoy was the only person he felt confident talking to, and now Jasper was sailing two thousand miles away from him.

"Don't worry, lad. Until you feel more comfortable, stay to yourself," the priest said.

Jasper was a wreck. His hands were shaking, and he was perspiring on the cool, cloudy day. He was struggling to breathe. His eyes had become shallow and fearful.

Father Hoy's heart poured out for him, but he felt a bit of the ol' "Back in the Saddle" would be just the ticket for him. "Here, take this." The Father handed Jasper a pint of whiskey. Jasper calmed a bit, but not much. "And take this one as well, in case there are any delays," the priest added, handing him a second pint.

"Thank you for everything, Father Hoy. If good ever comes from all of this, it'll be because of you," said Jasper after regaining his composure. The two embraced, and then Jasper silently turned and walked to the ship. Once he began to walk away, Jasper didn't look back.

Father Hoy watched as Jasper boarded the ship and waited for it to cast off before he turned to head home.

BOOM! A tattered football bounced off Father Hoy's forehead, accompanied by laughter from a group of children. The Father toed the ball, then faked an aggressive defense, keeping it away from the kids. A roar of cheers welcomed the new competition! Down the road they headed, in a fierce take-away battle. Father Hoy always gave the boys more than they could handle.

CHAPTER X
Dianna Sue

On this voyage, Jasper became keenly aware of the advantage of first-class over third-class, but he didn't have the nerve to upgrade his ticket. The thought of conversing terrified him. His third-class accommodation was a sleeping hammock in a small room with twenty-six other people. It was strictly functional – just a spot to sleep and set your bag. He may have been lucky not to have a bag. The travelers that did have one were wise to hold on to it as they slept.

Soup and bread were brought to the sleeping quarters, but he wasn't hungry. His appetite had all but abandoned him, and the number of people made him feel apprehensive.

During the day, he couldn't avoid the other passengers. The first night in the hammock the room was hot and crowded – he got no sleep at all. Exhausted, he crawled out of the hammock and wandered the ship, looking for a better place to rest.

On the second deck, he found a lifeboat with a loosely secured cover. After assuring he was alone, he crawled into the boat. It was dark, and he was, at last, alone. He took a long draw off the first pint of Father Hoy's whiskey and closed his eyes; sleep took him away.

To maintain his solitude, he wandered the deck at night and slept during the day. Late in the morning, when there were fewer people, he would head back to his assigned sleeping quarters to have some bread and soup, then slip back into his lifeboat to sleep.

May 15th, 1915

On the third day he ran out of whiskey. He was sure he couldn't function without it, but Jasper didn't panic. He had lost his nerve but not his intelligence. He had a plan. He found a door on the second deck that led to the kitchen, and waited outside for a server to walk out. Jasper stopped a young black woman as she was leaving the kitchen. "Excuse me, Miss."

The young woman was startled at first. She wanted no trouble with some dingy man. Then she saw his face, and her heart softened. She could see he was a broken man, and in her world she had experienced a few.

"Yes, sir?" she replied, still a bit suspicious.

"My name is Jasper P. Whittington III. May I ask yours?"

His reply shocked her. Most people just weren't that polite.

"Dianna Sue," she cautiously answered.

Jasper reached into a pocket, pulled out two one-dollar bills, and held them up.

"If you can bring me a bottle of whiskey, I'll give you two dollars: the first one now and the second when you bring it to me."

Dianna's eyes widened.

"If you got two dollars, why do you need me?" she asked.

Jasper froze. He didn't want to have a conversation but needed an ally.

He explained, "It's difficult for me, you see. People make me anxious. I'll be honest with you: I can't even sleep in my quarters. I sleep in a lifeboat just to be alone. I sleep all day so I can be alone at night. My apologies, Miss, but I'm just a bundle of nerves."

Dianna's eyes began to show concern. "What happened to you, sir?"

"I was on the Lusitania when it was attacked and I ..." Jasper's voice stuck in his throat, he was unable to continue. Instead, he looked away, out over the water.

All suspicion left the girl's face and was replaced with compassion. This man had lived through her greatest nightmare. After a short silence Dianna asked, "Which lifeboat?"

She agreed to his request and then went to the lifeboat every morning to see if he had enough food and whiskey for the rest of the trip.

May 19th, 1915

At 4:00 p.m. the next day the ship entered New York Harbor as Dianna Sue brought Jasper his meal. "We're approaching the Statue of Liberty, Mr. Whittington. Come have a look!" she exclaimed. She had seen it at least a dozen times but still enjoyed the sight. Her ancestors, coming from Haiti, saw it for the first time some two generations back. It was one of her mother's first memories.

Groggy and somewhat hungover, Jasper crawled out of the lifeboat. On his way to Europe he had missed the statue. Seeing it now he felt a moment of peace, but it wasn't enough to overcome his fear and anxiety.

When they reached the dock, Jasper stood alone, watching the ship moor and the passengers disembark. The calm he had felt earlier dissipated and his anxieties returned. He went back to the lifeboat, pulled out his bottle, and gulped down the last sip.

Jasper pulled out a hundred-dollar bill. When his suit was returned in Ireland, he had removed one of the three to give to Father Hoy. He felt the Father wouldn't have accepted it, so he opened the Bible he used for services to John 3:16 and placed it there. Jasper knew the Father would find it by Christmas.

Now, with one bill stashed back, he clutched the other in his hand and waited by the servants' exit. After a time, Dianna walked out in her street clothes and seemed pleasantly surprised to see Jasper waiting for her.

"Mr. Whittington, you're still aboard!" she said with a smile. She seemed aglow, happy to be home; she would soon see her family.

"I wanted to thank you again for your care and encouragement. Please give your family my best regards and best of luck in the future." Jasper reached out his hand to shake hers. She felt something touching her palm and assumed it was a generous one-dollar tip. Jasper turned and walked away. As he walked down the boarding plank, he heard a joyous scream and laughter come from Dianna.

In Cobh, Ireland, the poor and unfortunate had a warm fire and a wonderful Christmas dinner. Father Hoy organized a neighborhood football team with new balls and their very own uniforms. Stateside, a small group of young black entrepreneurs started an insurance group with a young woman who would eventually become the first black businesswoman in Harlem.

Without realizing it, Jasper had turned the loss of the Clemmens and the fear that held him so tightly after the torpedo attack into happiness. Jasper P. Whittington III had made the world a better place.

May 20th, 1915

After deboarding the ship, he walked to the exchange kiosk and changed his last hundred-dollar bill for tens. He felt it would be less conspicuous, and a ten was the largest denomination most businesses would accept. He stopped by the Levi Strauss store and bought a light jacket, a white button-down collar shirt, fresh long johns, a pair of jeans, socks, brown ankle-high boots, and a brown Fedora hat. He then went to the nearest hotel and paid extra for a room with a private bath. As Mrs. Clemmens would say, he was quite ripe after sleeping in a lifeboat for seven days.

He wanted to beat the crowds so he requested room service for his meals. In the morning breakfast was brought promptly at sunup. After eating, he left his old clothes in the hotel room, hoping someone else would put them to good use.

He then headed to Grand Central Station to find a train back to the western frontier. On the way, he stopped by a drugstore and bought ten half-pint bottles of Jim Beam whiskey. The man at the counter explained it would be cheaper to buy a bigger bottle, but Jasper felt it would be best not to have all his eggs in one basket. He also picked up a small leather satchel to carry them in.

Ninety-six dollars and twenty-five cents. That was the cash Jasper was carrying on the train from New York to Louisville, Kentucky, in his not-so-secret pocket. It had been twelve hours since Jasper had eaten, but the stations where the train stopped were just too busy for him to get off. So instead, he quietly drank himself into a stupor.

CHAPTER XI
Koen Van Haaften

May 21st, 1915

    When Jasper woke it was freezing! Man! Someone needed to start a fire. When he opened his eyes, to his horror, he was underwater. A woman with a child in her embrace floated by. The woman's legs were twisted outward. The baby's neck was clearly broken, and its head drooped down to the waist. Both were dead! His face and hands grew numb from the cold. It was becoming difficult to move. Worse yet, he needed air. He could taste the salty brine, and his lungs burned.

    He looked around and saw charred bodies, some broken and twisted, and others looking as if they were only asleep. All are floating in a sea full of debris from the sunken ship. Jasper looked up and saw the bright sun streaming down through the ocean water. The surface couldn't have been more than twenty feet away.

    He clawed his way upward to reach the air. His lungs were burning like fire. But the more he struggled, the slower he moved. The water around him felt thick. He was getting closer but was becoming desperate and began to panic.

He should reach the surface in one more stroke, but suddenly he could no longer move. He turned to see the girl he had tried to rescue, clinging to a deck fragment. Her one eye was open and her mouth quivered. She said, "Come with us, Jasper, it's your calling!"

Oddly, Milo and Gladys Clemmens swam up to join her. Staring with dead eyes, they clawed at him. Heartbreak and panic overwhelmed him. No longer able to keep it in, Jasper screamed! As he drew another breath his lungs filled with saltwater. Death was calling him! He shook uncontrollably and opened his mouth to scream again but nothing came out.

"Wake up! Wake up!" Jasper opened his eyes to see a man standing over him, shaking him violently by the arm. "Good Lord, have mercy, son!" said the man. "You fixin' to bring the man up in here, and ya damn sure don't want that!"

"Sorry," mumbled Jasper, "I was having a bad dream."

Jasper's eyes focused on the man, who looked to be about 40 but with a lot more wear. He was skinny as a rail, and his tattered clothes hung on his thin frame, making him look like a scarecrow. His matted blond hair and stubbly beard were filling in with gray. Through the beard and bushy eyebrows glared seafoam green eyes. Jasper had never seen anyone with eyes that color. They were otherworldly. But the man's sincere, toothless grin definitely brought him back down to earth.

"I'm thinking it was a bit more than just a bad dream," said the man. "What in the hell is a-goin' on with you?"

"I was on a ship that got torpedoed. Ever since then, I've been having nightmares," answered Jasper, rubbing his forehead as a mighty hangover took hold. He started to panic when he realized he was no longer on the train. "Where am I? Where's my bag? What in the hell's going on?!"

"Easy, buddy. You're in jail. The deputy and the jailer carried you in about three hours ago. They probably got your stuff."

Jasper immediately reached into his pocket and felt for his money. It was there. A slight sense of relief came over him. He knew it wasn't a good time to pull it out and count it.

"Jail?" asked Jasper.

"That's right," the man answered.

"Why am I in jail?" Jasper was befuddled.

"Drunk and disorderly! One of my favorites. This here is the best drunk tank on the Norfork Southern. Since it's just me and you here, we'll be standing before the man in the morning."

"Where is here, and who is the man?" asked Jasper.

"Ohhh, son! When they brought you in, you were drunker than Cooter Brown. No wonder you don't remember. They had to carry you off the train. You're in Louisville, and the man is Judge Brock." he paused and asked, "What do you mean torpedoed?"

"I was on the Lusitania," Jasper quietly answered.

The man's eyes widened as he exclaimed, "Shit fire to save matches! No wonder you spook so easy." Extending his hand, the man introduced himself. "I'm Koen Van Haaften. My pa's pa came over from Holland, so that kinda makes me Dutch. Ain't got no wooden shoes, though!"

Koen said that often and always made himself laugh.

"I'm Jasper P. Whittington III," he replied, reaching out to meet his handshake.

Koen froze. His smile washed away as he studied Jasper's face.

"Where you from, Jasper?" his tone became serious.

"Oklahoma."

"I know'd Oklahoma since before it was a state. Whereabouts in Oklahoma?" asked Koen, releasing his hand.

"Pryor. I've lived there all my life," answered Jasper, still clearing the cobwebs.

"You got any kin in Ada?"

"I ain't got no kin. I grew up in an orphanage. Why?"

Koen took a moment to ponder the weight of the next words that would come out of his mouth. "I know'd a man there that carried the same name."

The response shook Jasper completely sober. He wasn't sure what to say or do. This was a new feeling. He'd never considered having kinfolk a possibility. He wanted to ask a thousand questions but was shocked to silence.

"And, from what I remember, ya'll share quite a likeness," added Koen.

"When was this?" asked Jasper, looking up to make eye contact.

"Oh, it was a while back – '96 or '97. I was doing a thirty-day stretch in county jail for helping myself to one of the Sheriff's chickens. In my defense, I didn't know it was his chickens.

"When you're in Pontotoc County Jail, they're going to get some use out of you. They had us swinging those idiot sticks, clearing roadsides from sunup to sundown! There were five of us on the work crew. The Deputy brought us back to the jail one evening, and there were five other men we'd never seen before. We asked their names, and it turned out it was the Jim Miller gang. They'd put a shotgun to the chin of an old farmer and blew his head off before robbing him.

"They all looked scared, but that Jasper fellow looked way out of place. He said he was doing day work for the farmer and had no ties with Jim's gang, but the law wasn't buyin' his story. Later that night, we heard a bunch of people on horses and buckboards pull up. The sheriff came in and had Jim and the rest of his boys stand with their backs to the bars. Him and a couple of other men tied their hands behind their backs before taking them out of the cell. And lord! What a ruckus was raised when they went outside. Screamin' and a-hollerin' like it was judgment day.

"Later on, the Sheriff brought us some grub. After that, it was so quiet that night you coulda heard a mouse fart. The Deputy released us the next morning. Nothin' was ever said outright, but from what I understood, the Pontotoc County Courthouse saved a few tax dollars."

After a long pause, Jasper asked, "They lynched all of them?"

"Yep. That was the rumor. Sorry to be the one to bring the bad news, especially since I didn't witness it. But I can't see it ending any other way," said Koen, shaking his head.

Sadly, Jasper responded, "I appreciate you being straight up and all." A new emotion took over his heart. The first family member he'd ever heard about had been lynched. Either as a murderer or as an innocent man. "If you don't mind, I think I'll shut my eyes a bit." Jasper wondered if he'd ever be able to fill the growing hole in his heart.

The jailer showed up in the morning with a loaf of bread and coffee. Jasper's nerves were a wreck. Aside from the shocking news about a possible family member being lynched by an angry mob, he was painfully sober. Jasper remained quiet during breakfast. "Let's go, boys!" said the jailer. He escorted the men to the outhouse to take care of their business and then to an outdoor sink to clean up for court.

By all accounts, the courtroom was small but well-appointed. A court reporter awaited them, and the jailer became the acting bailiff. Otherwise, the courtroom was empty. The judge's chamber door opened, and the newly converted bailiff announced, "All rise! The court of Jefferson County is now in session, the honorable Philip K. Brock presiding."

Before sitting, Judge Brock looked down at the short court docket. Without speaking, he waved Jasper and Koen to the bench. The two men stepped closer. Koen seemed quite at ease in the courtroom and even greeted the judge with a nod and smile. Jasper, on the other hand, was silent and obviously shaken. Yet another unplanned first. He was standing before a judge. The bailiff took a seat.

"You two men stand before the court accused of the criminal misdemeanor of public drunkenness and disorderly conduct. How do you plead?" asked the judge.

"Guilty, your honor! Guilty as the day is long!" declared Koen.

"And you are?" asked the judge, looking down his nose.

"Koen Van Haaften, judge."

"A simple 'guilty' or 'not guilty' will suffice, Mr. Van Haaften. There is no need for a colorful commentary." Looking over to Jasper, the judge asked, "Mr. Whittington?"

"Yes, your honor."

"Mr. Whittington, how do you plead to the drunk and disorderly charge?"

"Guilty, your honor." Jasper kept his gaze straight forward so as not to antagonize the court.

Jasper appeared educated and well-spoken. His mannerisms set Judge Brock back a bit.

"Mr. Whittington, what brings you to my otherwise peaceful and law-abiding borough?"

"Just trying to make it back to Oklahoma, your honor."

"And what awaits you in Oklahoma?" asked the judge.

"Sorry, your honor, but I don't rightly know," answered Jasper, who was becoming nervous from the interaction.

"You need to elaborate, Mr. Whittington, before the court can consider your sentence." The judge urged Jasper to continue.

"Well, I grew up in a State Home, but for the last four years, I lived with some folks on a nearby farm," Jasper paused. He hadn't thought of Mr. and Mrs. Clemmens' kind ways in almost a month. His voice jumped back into his throat. For the first time, he was homesick. Tears began rolling down his cheeks. "And I just found out. I may have some kin there."

"I understand," the judge softened. "Now, specifically, why are you in Louisville?"

"I was on my way to battle the Hun, sir. But the ship I was on was sunk by the Germans before I got to England. That was enough war for me, your honor. I just want to hang my hat in a peaceful place. For me, that's Oklahoma. I . . ." Jasper fell silent, as did the rest of the courtroom.

"Son, you were on the Lusitania?" asked the judge softly.

"Yes, your honor. And I know I've had enough of war. I just want to go home."

"Do you have enough money to get you to Oklahoma without a vagrancy charge?"

"I do, your honor," answered Jasper.

"The court is dismissing the charges held against Mr. Whittington and releasing him on his own recognizance," the judge declared with a slam of his gavel.

"Mr. Van Haaften, the court finds you guilty as charged. I'll give you the option of paying a five-dollar fine or 30 days in county."

Before the gavel slammed, Jasper spoke up, "Your honor, is it possible that I might pay Mr. Van Haaften's fine? I could use the company on the way home. I'll pay for his fare. There will be no hoboing."

"Mr. Van Haaften, were you planning to go to Oklahoma?" asked Judge Brock.

"After this recent turn of events, yes, your honor, I am bound for Oklahoma," Koen chimed.

Judge Brock's demeanor softened.

"The accused has elected to pay the fine. In lieu of these new circumstances, the five dollars will be considered court fees, and all charges will be dropped." Before slamming the gavel he added, "Bailiff, after this preceding, please escort these two gentlemen to the diner and see that they are well fed, courtesy of the Jefferson County Courthouse."

Down came the gavel, and Judge Brock stood.

"All rise!" called the bailiff.

The judge readdressed Jasper. "Don't give up on life, son. There is a reason you're still with us. God has plans for you. Don't miss that opportunity because you were in a drunk tank."

"Thank you, your honor," Jasper quietly answered.

Koen stood silent. He hadn't heard a word said to Jasper after the judge released them. He only picked up on talk of a free meal and a free ride to Oklahoma. Koen was smiling.

Judge Brock's suggestion of sobriety lasted about thirty minutes, long enough for Jasper to grab his bag and get on the train to St. Louis. Mr. Van Haaften turned out to be good for the trip. He understood Jasper was easy to overwhelm. Even too much comfort could be difficult for him, so Koen would only lend it in the smallest of doses. He was the company Jasper needed.

CHAPTER XII
Ada

May 23rd, 1915

After arriving in Oklahoma City they changed trains, bound for Ada. They disembarked there with one bag between them, carried by Koen, clanking with empty bottles. To combat his ever-increasing sobriety, Jasper suggested they find a general store to replenish the stock.

Evans Hardware was next to the train station and Jasper and Koen walked into the store looking like two men who had just gotten out of jail, gotten off a long train ride, and were more than a little hungover because they just did and were.

Hearing the front door, the clerk came out of the back. He had a round, red face and was about the size of Mr. Clemmens' tractor. His girth surprised the boys.

"How can I . . ." The man froze in his tracks, and his eyes narrowed suspiciously. "Where ya'll comin' in from?" he asked with an unfriendly tone.

"OKC as of late," Koen answered flatly.

The man responded curtly. "Looky here, we don't run no soup line. You boys move along."

Jasper placed his clinking bag on the dark-stained oak counter and asked, "May I turn in these empties if I buy some more?" while pulling out seven empty half-pint bottles.

"I'll give you a penny each," answered the clerk.

"Why, it's three cents a bottle in Kentucky!" exclaimed Koen.

"Welcome to Oklahoma, old man," said the clerk. "Are we going to do this deal or not?" as he looked at Koen askance.

"Hum," Koen said, before walking out the front door.

"That's fine. And give me twelve half-pints of Jim Beam," said Jasper.

"I only have Old Crow in half-pints," said the man, reaching behind the counter.

"That's fine," repeated Jasper, wanting to leave. The clerk was the kind of man he didn't want to be around.

They finished the transaction, and outside Jasper saw Koen walking from behind the store.

"Where'd you go?" he asked.

"Outhouse. I had to drop off some groceries," Koen said with a mischievous smile. "Let's go talk to the sheriff. He may have some information on this other Whittington, but we have to tread lightly."

"It's been almost twenty years, Koen. What makes you think the same sheriff is still around?" asked Jasper.

"If'n he ain't dead he's still here." responded Koen.

"These are good ol' boys around here. You know, like that jackass running that hardware store. A new sheriff might stir something up. That isn't good for business. That's how some small towns operate."

The sheriff's office was located caddy-corner from the store. The two men approached, but Koen stopped a couple of steps short.

"You know, Jasper, this is the kinda thing I normally avoid." It was the first time Jasper had seen Keon with a solemn face. It made Jasper smile.

"Come on, now. We're free and clear. Besides, I need you to do the talking."

Reluctantly, Koen turned the glass doorknob, and the two walked into the office. They saw a large collection of rifles and revolvers secured and mounted on the opposite wall, along with a large coil of hemp rope. A heavy iron safe stood in the corner with its door closed, keeping its secrets. On the right, a trophy mountain lion stood, frozen in time, with its paw on a porcupine. Tacked to the wall, behind the sheriff's desk, a mass of yellowed newspaper clippings was on display. One headline read, "Jim Miller Gang Lynched - Justice Served." An elderly sheriff sat at the desk. He wore a white Stetson hat with a shiny gold badge pinned to a heavily starched white shirt.

As the two entered the room, the sheriff raised his head and rose out of the squeaky old chair to introduce himself. "I'm Sheriff Ed Carlson. What can I do for you boys?"

Koen and Jasper stood quietly for a moment as they took in the scene. Jasper didn't want to speak, and Koen was shaken up a little. He recognized the sheriff from almost twenty years before.

"Well?" probed Sheriff Carlson.

"I'm Koen Van Haaften and this here is Jasper Whittington. We are lookin' for some kin what mighta passed through here a while back. He had the same name – Jasper Whittington."

The sheriff's curiosity was replaced with suspicion. His eyes narrowed as he looked at Jasper. He cleared his throat and asked, "Don't you talk, boy?"

When a terrified Jasper was about to speak, Koen interrupted, "He's a mute, sheriff. He wanted me to do the talking for him."

The sheriff responded flatly as he turned to sit back down, "Whittington? Never heard of him. Is he from here?"

"Not sure, sheriff. We know'd he's from Oklahoma, but that's all we know," offered Koen.

"Well, there ain't nobody around here by that name and never has been." Sheriff Carlson was studying the two with a threatening glare, waiting for their response. The look frightened them.

The sheriff continued in a threatening tone, "I saw ya'll leave the station. Where ya headed?"

"Marlow, sheriff. I got kinfolk there. I reckon that's where I'll settle in. This here was just a long shot, sir. We'll be on our way," said Koen in a rush, taking Jasper by the arm. "We're much appreciative, sheriff! We'll be heading out now."

They walked out the door. Jasper found his voice and whispered, "He's lying."

Koen swung around to face him. "We are gonna buy our fares to Marlow and never come back to Ada. I don't want to see us on the wrong end of a rope!"

"But he's lying," repeated Jasper as Koen pulled him towards the station.

Jasper and Koen sat side by side in the passenger car, awaiting departure to Marlow, an hour or so west. Jasper reached for the whiskey, but Koen said they shouldn't drink a drop until Ada was behind them.

The train car heated up as the late spring sun climbed higher into the clear sky.

"Why Marlow?" asked Jasper as he wiped the sweat off his brow.

Koen responded, "Well, I know there's a station in Marlow, and I figured we needed to get out of town soon. It looked like that damn sheriff was beginning to see us as a problem." The train lurched forward and started west. "Jasper, that sheriff wouldn't a thought twice of stringing us up had we'd stayed in town after sundown. He's the king of Ada, and he aims to keep it that way."

The two men sat quietly, pondering the thought of being hung and buried in an unmarked grave in Ada, Oklahoma. Realizing Koen just saved his hide, Jasper gave him a half pint of whiskey.

Later that afternoon in Ada, the store owner stepped out to relieve himself of three Dr. Peppers and a pork sandwich. Still on the back porch, he slipped, fell, and rolled down the steps. Someone had left a smelly deposit on the top step. The store owner let out a tirade that still lives in the lore of Ada, Oklahoma. But that was nothing compared to what he said when he found someone had tied the outhouse door closed with a piece of baling wire.

CHAPTER XIII
Marlow

An hour later, Jasper and Koen stood on the platform at the Marlow train station. They were exhausted. Trains, fear, and whiskey had drained the fight out of them.

"Let's get a room," said Jasper, looking across the way at the Open Arms Hotel.

"I'm plum tuckered out," added Koen.

The men cleaned up in the community bath and settled into their room that evening. They drank their whiskey and ate the ham and bread that Jasper had picked up at the grocer. Both men laughed out loud when Koen told Jasper what he had done to the brash store owner. Small talk ensued until they both grew sleepy. Though they hadn't talked about it, the brush with death in Ada was the last thing Jasper thought about as they fell asleep.

In the morning, they rose and took the opportunity to use Marlow's first and only new-fashioned indoor toilet. After a good washing up, they went down to the White Rock Cafe for breakfast – coffee and a plate of flapjacks.

Finishing his last bite, Jasper spoke. "Look, Koen. I'm sticking around. If that man was family, I might have some more kin around here. You know, after spending this time with you, I feel better. I should plant myself and do some recuperating."

Jasper's words warmed Koen's heart but also concerned him. "Are you sure that's a good idea?" he asked.

"Don't worry about me, Koen. I'll keep an eye out," Jasper replied.

The men sat, not speaking for a moment. They watched the waitress deliver a plate of flapjacks to the table beside them. A car sputtered and rattled down the street.

"I've been planning to head out west, maybe California," said Koen. "I hear it has good weather and cheap living."

After a pause, Jasper asked, "Do you need some money?"

"Shit yes, I need money!" scoffed Koen. Both men laughed aloud.

"I've still got forty-six dollars and seventy-five cents," said Jasper, reaching in his pocket. "Take twenty," he said, handing Koen two tens.

The generous offer silenced Koen. He took a moment to compose himself.

"You sure?" he finally got out.

"Koen, you have helped me more than you'll ever understand. You spoke for me, kept me out of jail, and even dodged the hangman's noose. We may never meet again. It would hurt me if you didn't take it."

Koen smiled, took the money, and poured a small amount of salt on the table, forming a small mound.

"This here's for luck," he said.

Now, Jasper was reasonably educated but never heard of such a thing. "What's that, Koen?" he asked.

"Press it," instructed Koen.

When Jasper pressed it, Koen discharged gas like a giant fattening hog! The cafe fell deadly quiet. All eyes were on them. Jasper laid down a one-dollar bill, which made for a very nice tip, turned, and walked out. Koen tipped his hat and followed him, with a goofy, toothless grin. The next day, Jasper and Koen headed to the train station. Koen was shocked by the astronomical price of five dollars and thirty-six cents for the passage to Los Angeles, but paid it anyway.

The men then went to the platform and waited for the train's departure. Koen spoke first.

"Jasper, I feel like I'm leaving here an indebted man. This is the first time I've had more than just a few bucks to my name, and I'm kinda having a tough time coming to terms with it."

"You need to stop with that mess, Koen. Just let me ask you one question. What kinda shape am I in now compared to when we met?" asked Jasper.

"Lord have mercy, son, you were wound up tighter than a two-dollar watch! I must admit, I had my concerns about you."

"And how about now?" asked Jasper.

"Well, there's been a calmness to you. I reckon I don't need to fret as much," said Koen.

"Thanks to you," said Jasper. "You brought the calmness back to me. I truly believe no one else could have done that for me. I will always owe you for what little sanity I have recovered. Now, what price would you put on that?"

The question silenced Koen for a good while. The two stood quietly, watching the railmen loading the coal for the long journey. The coal chute was pulled away, the whistle blew, and porters stepped off the train to assist passengers aboard.

"Alright, dag-nabbit! Let me get on this train before one of us starts snot-bubblin'," Koen said, breaking the uncomfortable quiet. The remark made Jasper smile. It seemed Koen always knew how to break up an awkward moment.

"Well, we'll be seeing ya!" he said, extending his hand.

"Koen, I shouldn't be going anywhere. If you head back this way, you look me up," said Jasper, shaking his hand.

"Well, we'll just have to see how things unfold. That being said, if I do, I will," Koen replied.

Koen tipped his hat, turned, and climbed the steps into the passenger car. At the top, he turned back and said, "Good times are comin', Jasper. You've paid your dues." The train let go of its brakes and lurched forward. Koen found his seat and waved from the window. For the first time in a week, Jasper was alone.

CHAPTER XIV
Cyrus Smith

Jasper spent two more nights in the Open Arms. He laid in bed trying to grasp his present situation. He couldn't believe it had only been a month since he'd left Pryor on his way to Europe. It felt like ten years. He looked back on who he was on his last day in Pryor, remembering the good townspeople who waved goodbye. Though still eighteen, he was a different man now.

Fear and loss still guided his every move. He was unable to speak to anyone comfortably. It was a new handicap for him. He feared loneliness but wanted to be left alone. His reason and intelligence remained with him, but in many cases it just created more anxiety. That's when the whiskey became medicine. He wasn't sure if the whiskey was what made his nightmares go away, but he decided to keep drinking, just in case.

On the third morning, he sat on the bench on the sidewalk in front of the hotel, trying to decide what to do. He knew his money wouldn't last and attending university was out of the question now that he could not tolerate crowds. He needed to find work and a place to stay, but couldn't maintain a normal workday.

As Jasper sat musing, a tall, thin man in a tight-fitting black suit and black tie approached from across the street. His eyes were pale blue, and his nose and chin tapered to fine points. His face was pitted with smallpox scars. He moved with subtle intent, and his gate was long and lumbering. He had a look that would make most children cross the street to avoid him.

"Morning, sir. My name is Cyrus Smith. And you?" the man said, extending his hand toward Jasper. On one of his fingers was a Masonic ring featuring the Knights Templar symbol.

The man's approach shocked Jasper, who was trying to avoid interaction with anyone. He reluctantly shook the man's hand and said, "I'm Jasper P. Whittington III."

"It's a pleasure, Mr. Whittington. May I ask why you're sitting out in front of the Open Arms this late in the morning? Don't you have a job?"

"Well, it appears I'm between opportunities," answered Jasper.

Even cleaned up, Jasper was quite a sight. "What happened to you, boy?" asked Cyrus.

"Well, it's a long story, mister. It's tough for me to be around people. I just get knotted up. So, if you don't mind, I'll need to move on," said Jasper, getting up and walking away.

"Allow me to explain why I ask," said Mr. Smith, rejoining Jasper as he walked slowly down the sidewalk. "I'm the mortician here in Marlow. I have other tasks to perform besides preparing loved ones to meet the Lord. I'm looking for a trustworthy man to perform a few routine tasks, one I can leave to his own devices. I have dealt with men in circumstances similar to yours. Now, I don't expect you to stay with me for twenty years. But for whatever time you decide to stay, I know you can be trusted. Would you be the kind of man I'm looking for?"

This stopped Jasper in his tracks. "What do you mean, men in similar circumstances?"

"You're an interesting lot, you boys hanging around the train station. You normally break down into two groups. There are career vagrants who stick together and survive on some gentle thieving. And then there's men like you, loners, just good men, down and out. I must say, for a man who deals mainly with the dead, I'm a pretty good judge of character."

Jasper appreciated men who spoke clearly and without pretense. He had planned to stay in town, at least for a while.

"What's the job?" asked Jasper.

"Walk with me, Mr. Whittington?" asked Mr. Smith.

"Well. . ." Jasper hesitated, "um, sure."

The men walked north on Railroad Street, parallel to the train tracks. They spoke of Jasper's tough, short life. Mr. Smith respected his need for solitude. After a quarter mile, they turned right and crossed the tracks.

"Marlow Cemetery" was neatly set in big block letters above the rod iron gate. On a brass plate fixed to the gate was a small sign. "Open, sunrise. Closed, sunset." The gate was open wide.

"One of your tasks will be to lock and unlock this gate," Smith explained.

Jasper looked left and right and was a little befuddled. He noticed there was no fence.

"Why?" he asked.

"The insurance company suggested we hire manned security and install a lockable gate for a better rate. I refer to this gate as our humble deterrent. We are just abiding by the rules in our own meager way."

The men entered the cemetery and strolled down the red dirt road through the shade of old elm trees. On the left was a small stone building. Mr. Smith unlocked the door and the two men entered a small room. There were two finely carved walnut chairs beside a small oval table. Light and fresh air streamed through a small frame window, which provided a view of the oldest part of the cemetery. On the table was an opened guest's registry. Later, Jasper was told that the list of recorded names was a great source of business.

"Please, have a seat, Mr. Whittington. I want to explain the duties required for this position."

"Yes, sir," replied Jasper.

"You seem to be a man with more than average intelligence, so I'll be frank with you. We mainly benefit by having a man on our payroll regardless of the tasks performed. The insurance company requires proof of employment. For that, I'll need a valid form of identification."

"Is a passport ok?" asked Jasper.

"Yes, that'll do nicely, Mr. Whittington. Now, we'll need you to take a few passes through the burial grounds nightly and, of course, lock and unlock the entrance gate at the appropriate times. It would be helpful if, during your walk, you would collect any rubbish you may come across. Now, if you happen upon any shenanigans, I can arrange for you to contact me by telephone in the Open Arms."

"Mr. Smith, I've never used a telephone," said Jasper.

"That's fine, Jasper. The hotel clerk will help you. Oh, may I call you Jasper?"

"Of course," Jasper replied.

"Good! And please, call me Cyrus. Let me show you the sleeping quarters."

The men rose and took a few steps to the only inside door.

"Here we are," said Cyrus. The tiny room had a small, iron-framed bed with a feather mattress. On it lay fresh, folded linens and an Army surplus blanket. A small wooden cross hung on the wall above the head of the bed. A small trunk was in the corner at the foot. "There's a water spigot by the outhouse, just out back. This will be yours for as long as you need it," said Cyrus waving at the room.

Strangely, Jasper found it inviting. He could make it work. "I'll take the job, sir," he said after a long pause. "Oh! What's the pay?"

"We'll start you at two dollars a week. You can put two meals daily on my tab at the White Rock Cafe. When you need to wash that linen or clothing, just bring it to the back entrance of the funeral home and drop it off. We'll take care of it. Will that work for you?"

"Fine by me, sir," answered Jasper.

"You'll be paid on Fridays. Do you need an advance?" asked Cyrus.

"No, sir. I'm set for now," said Jasper, patting his pocket.

"Smith's Funeral Home is two blocks west of Highway 81 on Comanche Street. Stop by if you need anything. If I'm not available, leave a message with my receptionist. Do you have any questions?" asked Cyrus.

"No, sir. I should be fine for now," said Jasper, looking around the room.

"Then I'll leave you to it. Contact me if you have any issues at all," Cyrus said, extending his hand, and the men shook on the deal.

"Mr. Smith, I truly appreciate your generosity. Giving me this opportunity is a great act of kindness." Jasper hesitated, then asked, "But why?"

"Oh! Well, I suppose I feel, but by the grace of God, go I. A man in my profession has a unique vantage point when summing up a lifetime. At the end of every funeral service, people either smile and relive fond memories, saying things like, 'I'll never forget what he did for me . . .' or 'She baked the best pecan pies!' or they say nothing and simply walk away, just a bit sadder. I found that the people who left the world in better shape were the most loved and celebrated. There's always someone in need and always someone who has the opportunity to help. I have somehow outlived my family, so now I reach out to help people like you. This, Mr. Whittington, is how I'll leave the world a better place."

The two stood silently, allowing a moment to solidify their words. It seemed they both understood the significance of their meeting. This was a pivotal moment. Jasper needed to define it, as a turn for the worse or for the better, but he wasn't quite sure and wondered if it even mattered. His ability to reason was beginning to fail. Life was no longer black and white. It had become only shades of grey. The words of Counselor Standish flashed into his head, "Your decisions can carry unanticipated consequences now that you're a man of means. I'm afraid your childhood is over." With this thought Jasper sat down on the unmade bed.

"Mr. Smith, if you don't mind, I'll need to sit and rest for a while. My head is beginning to swim," said Jasper.

"Very good, Mr. Whittington. I'll leave you to it. Here are the keys. If there's anything at all I can help with, just let me know," replied Cyrus. He smiled and left the room. Jasper stretched out on the bed and closed his eyes.

When he opened his eyes, he found himself in the arms of a beautiful young woman. Though he didn't recognize her, she seemed familiar. Her sweet smile and loving arms comforted him. She spoke, but he didn't understand what she was saying. Nevertheless, her words gave him a peace and comfort he had never known. He slowly realized he was being held in her arms like a baby, and she was smiling at a man sitting across the room. He, too, looked familiar. He was a skinny man wearing a white button-down shirt with a loose-fitting black jacket and slacks. He wore a black flapjack pulled down to the side. He smiled and said, "Welcome home, son."

The words faded as Jasper awoke. Dusk had fallen. The cicadas had changed their song from a long, loud rattle to a steady cry, oscillating up and down – a sure sign summer was near. It was getting dark outside, and there were no lights in his room. He stepped out to the receiving room and saw that Cyrus had left an oil lamp and matches for him. He decided to take his first round of the evening, lighted the lamp, and stepped out into the darkness that had completely taken over.

Marlow was a sleepy little town that grew quiet on weekday evenings. He followed the dirt roads and paths through the cemetery. It was very peaceful. He felt completely alone, but in a good way.

He came across ten or so graves fenced off from the rest. By looking at the dates, he could see it was a section reserved for children. As he read the tombstones, he noticed that none of them were dated more than ten years.

Suddenly, he froze in his tracks. One tombstone read: Pierre Montclair, Born March 3rd, 1915, and Died March 3rd, 1915. Shot to death by Germans. "But that's not possible," thought Jasper. Then, muffled infant cries came from the graves. The cries of older children joined in. The soil on top of the graves broke, then tumbled aside as small hands, then arms reached out. An earsplitting horn bellowed from a steamship as the children crawled out of their graves. Jasper covered his ears as they chanted, "Jasper, come with us! It's your calling!"

Jasper screamed himself awake. The room was now pitch black. He scrambled for his bag and took a long pull on a fresh bottle of Old Crow as his eyes adjusted to the dim starlight. He slowly stood and stretched. His eighteen-year-old body was tight and sore. He was moving like a man twice his age.

He stepped out to the reception and saw an oil lamp with matches sitting next to the registry. He sat and lighted the lamp. Though he certainly wasn't looking forward to it, it was time for his first security walk. After a little more liquid courage, he took the lamp and headed out.

All seemed still and quiet in the cemetery. The whiskey had done its work. He was no longer shaking. The cool evening air was a relief from the hot, humid late afternoon. During his walk he felt his bones relax. His anxiety faded as he wandered about the dark graveyard. The fear was still there, but it was no longer dominant. Other than an occasional bark from a distant dog or rustle from a raccoon, the night was his. Now, he could do what he did best: think.

What would be the effect on him if he actually met a real relative? How would he deal with establishing a completely different and new relationship? Would it help give him the peace he so desperately needed, or would he end up an unwanted embarrassment to an estranged family? Was it worth the risk? Now he was in a manageable situation. For better or worse, meeting family would start a new phase in his life, and he knew there would be unintentional consequences. Father Hoy's words came back to him, "Don't worry, lad. Till you feel more comfortable, just stay to yourself." Jasper decided that he was in a good position to heal for a while. When he felt stronger he might pursue his past.

By predawn, Jasper was feeling better. He had made it through his first night in the cemetery. Walking back to his room, he felt relaxed, like he did after long conversations with Koen or Mr. Clemmens. He made his bed and climbed in. He took one last drink to fend off the nightmares, and slept peacefully.

Jasper's mind grew calmed a bit as days turned to weeks. Then weeks to months. He established a routine for his walks. There were several park benches along the paths where he strolled, and there were two he always stopped at. He would take a little sip of whiskey at each one, ponder some, then move on. Near one of those benches, a prominent tombstone read:

Seaman Robert E. Lee Burris

Born May 1st, 1880, Died 15 February 1898.

"Gave his life in service to his country aboard The USS Maine."

The nights were beginning to get lonely. In fear of falling into another bout of melancholy, Jasper decided to look up Robert E. Lee Burris in the local archives at the library. Getting to know the person in the grave he saw every night would give that old soul a sense of presence and help Jasper with his loneliness.

Soon he had the details memorized. Robert came from a large family of twelve. At age ten, his family headed west from Georgia to Oklahoma's Red River. He was Evelyn and Andrew Jackson Burris' sixth child of ten. His siblings were John Walker, William Franklin, Leta Evelyn, Joe Henry, Mary Elvira, Anna Bell, Thomas Jefferson, and James Obadiah. Though he never attended school, his older siblings and mother taught him to read and write. At age seventeen, he enlisted in the Navy to see the world. He never married.

Jasper would casually address his grave each evening, "Good evening, Seaman Burris." In time, Jasper started having conversations with the lost sailor. He spoke of his time in the State Home and with the Clemmens Family. He spoke of his dreams of becoming a fighter pilot and how they were shattered before he got to fly, but his voice left him every time he tried to explain details of the violent event that changed his life.

One night, as he rose from the bench to finish his rounds, he heard a distant voice, "Call me Bobby."

Jasper froze. In all the time he had spent in the cemetery, it was the first he had heard any other voice but his own. Though his eyes were fixed on Robert's, well, Bobby's tombstone, his peripheral vision picked up a bright blue glow on his left. Jasper slowly turned and saw a young man in a naval uniform sitting beside him on the bench.

The man's uniform was perfect! Not one crease or wrinkle. He was clean-shaven, and his black shoes maintained a high gloss shine. He would have made any other seamen sitting next to him look shabby. As he peered back at Jasper through the dim light, he casually pulled long draws on his Turkish meerschaum pipe. As he exhaled, the smoke gathered around his face, then quickly disappeared.

The pipe was a beautiful carving of a sailor's head that would wink if you looked closely. It was well worn from use, fading from a parchment white to a rich dark purple. Jasper found the aroma of the pipe pleasing. It reminded him of the quiet evening air on the top deck of the Lusitania as they had steamed across the ocean.

Bobby appeared, just as many specters in novels he read, in colors of a pale, moonlight white with many shades of transparent blue. Oddly, Jasper felt no fear or apprehension; instead, he felt safe, and had a sense of belonging. He also had a strong desire to hear what Bobby had to say. He took a deep breath and said,

"Ok, Bobby."

"Jasper, why you walking around in a graveyard?" Bobby's Oklahoma accent was strong.

"Well, it's my job," said Jasper.

"Ok, ok. Now stop that! You know what I'm askin'. How'd you end up working nights in a graveyard?"

Jasper sat quietly for a moment, choosing his words.

"A while back, I started my first big adventure. I had the money, a good plan, and a strong desire to succeed. But something horrible happened on my way, something I just wasn't prepared for. I saw things no man should ever see." Jasper stopped momentarily. The memory of the attack was something he didn't want to talk about. He quickly changed the subject and said, "Looks like you died in combat. That must have been terrifying."

"Well, the truth is, the night before the attack I went to Havana to see about a gal. It seems I might have had more than my share of rum and walked off the dock on my way back to the ship and drowned. The attack was later that morning. My C.O. listed me as a casualty so Mama and Daddy would get the policy check." You could almost hear Bobby smiling as he told the story.

"Still, it's an awful shame to have to die so young," said Jasper.

"Why's that? We all die," said Bobby.

"But you were so young. Don't you think you missed out on life?" asked Jasper.

"I didn't miss out on life. I lived, and then I died. That's what everyone does. Now I'm here. This is where I should be. There's an old, established order that no living man could ever understand, and when you're called, you go. You only have control over how well you live your life. That's how you will be remembered. The memory of you in folks' hearts and minds is how you continue living after death. I'm sure the truth about how I died will eventually come out, but there are enough good memories about me that my folks will be laughing and talking about it for generations. Now, that's a life well lived."

Jasper sat silently before Bobby's grave, folding Bobby's words into his own thoughts.

"Dying so young, don't you feel you've missed out on anything?" asked Jasper.

"Well, I do miss Mama's fried chicken. And I miss my Uncle Oglethorpe's tall tales, but no, I didn't miss out on anything. I reckon everything kinda went as planned. Why do you keep asking me if I missed out on something?"

"I don't know. I thought people who died before finishing what they wanted to do would have regrets like they missed out on something," said Jasper.

Bobby sighed; he was becoming frustrated. "Jasper, no one dies before they've finished their life. Death means the journey is complete. You didn't die during that torpedo attack 'cause your journey ain't done. That's the same reason you didn't get hung in Ada. Your story is still being told. Things may get better – hell, things may get worse, or it could be the end of the journey. Whatever it is, you are precisely where you need to be, at this particular place and at this particular time. You need to check all that pain and get on with living. The past is deader than a Christmas goose. You got to turn your eyes forward, Jasper."

"Turn my eyes forward to what?" asked Jasper, staring straight ahead.

"Man, alive! 'Turn my eyes forward to what?' Ain't that the question! Heck! I don't know. I don't think anybody knows. But what I do know is you'll never answer that question while you're drowning in the past."

His words echoed and faded away. Jasper turned his head towards Bobby, but he was gone. The calm, quiet night air returned. A distant dog barked. Jasper sat alone on the bench.

For weeks, Bobby's words swirled in Jasper's head. After that night, he had a constant, comforting feeling he wasn't alone. His anxiety was slowly crumbling away. It was becoming easier for him to interact with people. He never spoke with Bobby again.

Jasper's life had become blissfully mundane. He began spending holidays with Cyrus and Miss Cleophina, Cyrus' full-time housekeeper. Christmas, Thanksgiving, and Easter were now enjoyable again. When the reception room, where Jasper was living, needed the space for services, he would head into town for a look-see. He'd fill the time picking up soap, toiletries, and whiskey at the RX.

Five years into Jasper's temporary position, Cyrus came with some big news. He had purchased property as an investment. It was a quarter-acre lot with a shotgun shack and an outdoor water pump and was only a few blocks from the cemetery. Cyrus asked Jasper if he would do him a favor and stay there to keep an eye on the place. Jasper offered up a little resistance but accepted. Two days later, he entered his new home and was very surprised to see a parlor with a divan and rocking chair, a kitchen with a sink, and a wood-burning stove. And best of all, through the kitchen window, he saw his very own outhouse. The bedroom had a wood frame bed with a fresh feather mattress, nightstand, and dresser drawers. It reminded him of a hotel room where he'd once stayed.

CHAPTER XV
Betty and Freddy

July 10th, 1925

Could it be possible? Ten years since he came to Marlow? New houses had popped up all around, and nobody seemed to notice Jasper much. His new home away from home was the public library. There was no need to buy books now; he could check them out. Sometimes he would sit and read there for hours. He didn't mind the company of people but still maintained his solitude. He was on good speaking turns with Miss Flippins, the librarian, who would also remind Jasper when it was time for a bath. He would catch an occasional movie but still thought the idea of men wearing paint on their faces and clobbering each other with sticks was a bit silly.

Marlow was booming! There was an Army post setting up nearby which would soon handle most of the Army's artillery training, creating many jobs. And the oil. Big oil companies and wildcat drillers had poured into southwest Oklahoma. Every square inch of that area and northern Texas smelled of oil and natural gas.

Fortunes were won and lost daily. Haliburton's Oil had become the new governing body in Marlow.

Apparently all brought on by those damn automobiles. What a strange, new world.

The war to end all wars had come and gone. Cyrus had been a busy man. Business flourished due to the Great War and the Spanish Flu, but seeing so many people struggle with their losses broke his heart. A great deal of Cyrus' profits were donated to the veterans' homes and the local widows and orphans fund. The townspeople appreciated his generosity, but being a mortician still came with a certain stigma. Cyrus spent most of his time alone or with Jasper. Sadly, he had left this world three weeks ago. Miss Cleophina found him in bed. He peacefully died in his sleep.

Jasper inherited the shotgun shack he lived in and a small but ample trust fund from Cyrus. The law firm handling Smith's estate was also tasked with managing Jasper's administrative and financial needs. A new, ornate fence was built around the cemetery, so a guard was no longer needed. But Jasper's love and gratitude for Cyrus drove him to continue his security walks.

The distance from Jasper's home to the cemetery was only a few hundred yards, so he never bothered to get a car. Every day, he passed a corner lot house on Nabor Street, beside the railroad tracks. There was a two-bedroom home with a root cellar in the front yard and a barn in the back. On the side of the house was an old walnut tree with tattered hemp ropes hanging from the lowest branch. The lot next to it was undeveloped, but it looked like crops had grown there. He began to observe the family living in the house. He would often see a little girl and boy playing in the yard. On occasion, he would see the young mother hanging out laundry or snapping green beans on the front porch, but he never saw the father.

One ice-cold December morning, as Jasper walked home from the cemetery, he saw the boy and girl standing next to the railroad tracks struggling with large buckets. They were shivering and weren't dressed warm enough for the weather. He supposed their mother must have been in the house. You could smell a pot of beans cooking, and Lord, they smelled good! Jasper decided to check on the children.

"Morning, children. Why are you standing out here with buckets?" asked Jasper.

"We're waitin' fer the eight-fifteen outta Chikasha!" said the boy, obviously the youngest of the two. He seemed quite proud of his detailed answer, though his older sister rolled her eyes.

She said, "The coalman on the eight-fifteen is the nicest! We ought to get at least a week's worth this morning."

"A week's worth of what?" asked Jasper.

"Coal, mister!" answered the boy with pride.

"The engineer always slows down right here, and Mr. Coalman shovels out coal for us. Mama says he's an agent of the Lord!" said the girl with great reverence.

A train whistle sounded in the distance, and the children perked up.

"Here they come!" they shouted in unison.

The girl looked at Jasper with a bit of concern. "You better go off and hide, mister. We don't know what Mr. Coalman will think with three of us out here," said the girl. "Oh! Unless you need some coal, too."

"Oh, I'm fine, children. I'll leave you to your task," said Jasper as he tipped his hat and headed home.

"Hey, mister!" shouted the girl. "I'm Betty! And this here's Freddy! He's named after Daddy, and I'm named after Mee-ma."

Jasper turned and answered, "I'm Jasper, it's a pleasure to meet you."

In five minutes, Jasper had entered his quiet home, removed his boots and hat, and went straight to the stove. It couldn't have been more than forty-five degrees in the house. He lit the paper and kindling preloaded in the stove. After it stoked up, he added wood. The tiny house would be livable in ten minutes.

He pulled out a can of Campbell's Pork and Beans, opened it, and placed it on the stovetop. He was eating like a bachelor. He didn't care much for the beans, but they sat pretty heavy and kept him full for a while. As he waited for them to heat up, he listened to the Catfish String Band on the radio blaring from the Widow Delbrook's house. She was just as sweet as she could be but dang near deaf. She lived three doors down.

Jasper finished his beans as the little house warmed from the fire. With his belly full he grew sleepy and headed for bed. He no longer dreaded closing his eyes. His nightmares had all but gone away. Though his hankering for drink had faded, he'd still take a shot before bed. The last thing he remembered before drifting off was the faces of the two children he spoke with that morning and the Catfish String Band singing "I'll Fly Away."

CHAPTER XVI
Evelynn

Two weeks later, on December 24th, Jasper was walking on Railroad Street after a long, cold night at the cemetery. Eighteen inches of snow had fallen in the past two days, and the temperature hadn't risen above freezing. When he passed the house on Nabor Street he would check to make sure smoke was billowing from the stove stack. Imagining the family huddled in the kitchen warmed his heart.

The mother's panicked voice rang from the house.

"Freddy!" she shouted. The front door burst open and she screamed, "Someone! Please help!"

Without hesitation, Jasper sprinted to the woman. Before he could ask, the mother cried frantically, "It's Freddy! He can't breathe!"

Jasper looked in the door and saw the boy lying on the kitchen floor. Little Betty sat at the table, sobbing with her face in her hands. Jasper ran to the boy and picked him up. The child wasn't breathing and his face had gone blue. No doctor could get here in time. Jasper looked at the mother and asked, "What ails him?"

"He's got something stuck in his windpipe! I can't get it out!" she said.

Jasper has been in tough spots before; he did not panic.

"We've got to clear his throat. Come with me," said Jasper. "He's gonna be alright, ma'am."

The mother followed them out the front door. Jasper carried the child to the front yard and roughly patted him on his back.

"Rub some snow on his face, ma'am; maybe the cold will help," said Jasper as the boy's face changed from blue to pale white. He was beginning to fade. With that, Jasper had an idea. He got behind the boy and wrapped an arm around his tiny waist. Jasper thrust his closed fist repeatedly into the boy's belly. On the third thrust, with a loud pop, a Humdinger bumble bee marble shot into the snow, followed by a deep inhale by Freddy. As the color returned to the boy's face, Jasper turned him around.

"You OK, boy?" he asked.

"My tummy hurts," said Freddy, wheezing.

"That's alright. You just . . ." Before Jasper finished his sentence, Freddy threw up in his face with the force that could knock a knot out of a two-by-four at fifty paces. The mother burst out in uncontrollable laughter and tears. Betty stood at the screen door, her own tears turning to laughter. After a stunned moment, Freddy joined in on the laughter, too. Jasper was hesitant about opening his mouth until he felt it was safe.

"Oh, bless you, sir! Bless you! Ya'll come to the kitchen and I'll clean you up," said the mother.

Jasper picked the boy up and followed the two ladies into the kitchen.

"Betty, put a bucket of water on the stove and take your brother's clothes off. I'll go get some fresh ones," the mother said.

Betty went to the indoor pump at the sink and filled the bucket. She struggled to lift it onto the warm stove and then added a couple chunks of coal to the fire. Betty looked at Freddy and silently motioned him to her. It was warmer by the stove. She unbuttoned her brother's shirt and then started untying his shoes. The mother came back with some folded clothes for Freddy, washcloths, and a clean, folded pair of men's Oshkosh overalls.

"When you finish wiping down your brother, take them fresh clothes and go sit on the divan – and get under a blanket. OK, sugar?" said the mother.

"Yes'um," said Betty.

"And you must be Jasper," she said, turning to him with a smile.

"Yes, ma'am. May I ask your name?" answered Jasper, a bit sheepish.

"Evelynn," she said, smiling. "Here's some fresh clothes to put on after you get cleaned up."

"Thank you, ma'am," said Jasper.

Evelynn went out of the kitchen and pulled the curtain closed to give him privacy.

"Oh! You can just leave those dirty clothes on the floor. I'll wash them later," she said through the curtain.

"There's no need, ma'am . . ." But Evelynn cut him off and said, "It's no bother, Jasper. Besides, it's the least I can do."

In ten minutes, they were all back at the table. Evelynn set everyone up with a bowl of beans and a big slice of cornbread. As children often do, Freddy experienced a miraculous recovery and devoured his lunch like he was in a competition. Betty watched and could only shake her head.

"Why do you eat like that, Freddy? I swear! You are a P-I-G pig! And right here, in front of company."

Freddy just rolled his eyes and shoved a big piece of cornbread in his mouth.

The interaction warmed Jasper's heart.

"Well, it is certainly nice to meet you, Jasper. The kids have been spying on you for a while and keeping me updated," said Evelynn, giving them a gentle side-eye. Now that the morning's excitement was over, the two finally got a chance to take a good look at one another.

Evelynn was small, no more than five feet and ninety pounds. Her hair was chestnut brown with a few premature gray streaks and was pulled into a bun. Her eyes were hazel with bright amber highlights that softly demanded your attention. She had a little button nose, no bigger than an acorn. Her lips gently curled up on the corners of her mouth.

This was Jasper's first eye-to-eye with someone for a long time. And she was lovely.

Evelynn was also taking in Jasper. She had only seen him from a distance, walking in black trousers and jacket, a dingy white shirt, and a black flapjack hat. Jasper spent most of his daylight hours sleeping, so at twenty-eight his skin was still fair and youthful. He had a slender face. His green eyes were full of emotion, revealing both pain and joy. And oh! Good Lord! That hair needs some attention, she thought to herself. And that beard has to go! As a matter of fact, he could use a good scrubbing down. He was a bit ripe!

"Jasper, what are your plans for tomorrow?" asked Evelynn, breaking the silence.

"Tomorrow?" asked Jasper.

"Yes. It's Christmas. If you have no plans, you must spend the day with us! The children would love it!" she said nodding toward the children. "We'll only have beans and fatback but you are more than welcome."

"Oh, please come stay with us tomorrow!" shouted Betty. Freddy vigorously agreed by nodding his head. He couldn't speak. He had so much beans and cornbread shoved in his mouth that he looked like a chipmunk.

"Land sakes, Freddy! You're gonna choke yourself! No one here wants to see the insides of your belly again," said Evelynn. The memory of the projectile vomiting hit all of them at once. Followed by a burst of laughter from everyone, less Freddy. He had his hand over his mouth, forcing beans and cornbread out of his nose. It was a disturbing yet funny sight.

Jasper agreed to spend Christmas Day with the family. He sat at the table and listened to the kids describe what Christmas was like at their house. As they spoke, Jasper and Evelynn occasionally made brief eye contact. Jasper sensed her interest, but there were a lot of unanswered questions. Namely, whose clothes was he wearing?

It was past Jasper's bedtime, and an unpreventable yawn took him over. Evelynn smiled.

"You seem tuckered out," she said.

"Yes, ma'am," answered Jasper. "When should I come calling, Mrs.?"

"Mender, Evelynn Mender," she said. "Mister?"

"Whittington, Jasper P. Whittington III," Jasper said with a bow.

"Late morning will do nicely, Mr. Whittington"

"I'm looking forward to it, Mrs. Mender," he smiled.

Jasper made the two-block walk home with his feet in the snow and his head in the clouds. It had been a long time since he had sat at a table with a family and laughed. For the first time in decades, his heartbeat now guided him. Man! She was really something! But then he stopped and looked down at his clothes.

Jasper entered his ice-cold home. The frost from his breath filled the air as he walked to the kitchen and loaded up the stove to start the fire. Slowly, the kitchen warmed. His thoughts returned to the family he'd spent the morning with.

"Not since Pryor . . ." he whispered aloud.

"Christmas!" he blurted.

Jasper gathered his hat and coat and headed back out. He hoped the grocers were still open.

CHAPTER XVII
The Glasby's

A seamless grey sky hung over Marlow that Christmas Eve. Relentless winds blew powdered snow into large drifts, reminding Jasper it was about as far as you could get from a warm spring day. Ahead of him was a three-block walk to Glasby's Grocer and Hardware store on Main Street. It took twenty minutes in the deep snow. He reached the entrance of the store where a holly wreath with red ribbons hung on the front door. He stomped his feet on the wooden sidewalk to clear off the snow.

Before entering, he glanced through the display window and saw a most pleasing sight. There were three men in chairs sitting around an old potbelly wood-burning stove. Mrs. Glasby was behind the counter putting away wares. Mr. Glasby was pouring whiskey into three porcelain-plated coffee cups. The mood was bright and warm. Jasper opened the door and walked in. His entrance was announced by ringing sleigh bells hanging on the inside doorknob.

"Hey! Merry Christmas, Jasper!" said Mrs. Glasby. The men in the room looked up with smiles and joined in the season's greetings.

"Thank you, Mrs. Glasby. And a Merry Christmas to you all!" said Jasper with a sincere smile and a bit of shyness.

"Would you like a touch of Christmas cheer?" Mr. Glasby asked, holding up the pint bottle.

"Well," Jasper hesitated. "Maybe just one," he said with a nod.

Mr. Glasby retrieved another cup from under the counter, poured in some black coffee and Jim Beam, and handed it to Jasper. He took a sip. The mix was hot and bitter but remarkably warming and comforting.

"Mrs. Glasby. May I ask your advice?" he asked.

"Of course, Jasper. How may I help?"

"A family has invited me to their home for Christmas. I would like to provide the fixin's for a nice dinner."

"Why, that's just lovely, Jasper. How many will there be for dinner?" she asked.

"Humm. Two adults and two children. And I want to make it truly special. These folks have kind of been on their own. I believe a big Christmas is well deserved," said Jasper with a big smile.

"Goodness, Jasper! You're certainly all aglow. Who will you be spending the holiday with?"

"Mrs. Mender and her two children, on Nabor Street," said Jasper.

"Well, isn't that wonderful? I know life has been hard on them since her husband disappeared. It's been six years now. And she still hasn't heard anything?" Mrs. Glasby asked.

"I wouldn't know, ma'am. We just met. Her little boy, Freddy, got himself in a pickle, and I helped them out. Mrs. Mender, out of gratitude, I suspect, invited me over for Christmas. That's about all I know."

"Well, her husband, Fred, shipped off to the Great War in '18 and never made it back," said Mrs. Glasby.

"Missing in action?" asked Jasper.

"No, not really. He sent Evelynn a letter from Baltimore saying his ship was being held at the port on account of the flu. He said he was a month out, but they never heard another peep. Oh, people speculated. Maybe the flu got him, or maybe he got mugged. There were criminals waiting at every port to rob men of their back pay. Me? I never trusted him much. He was always drinking, and Lord! He was a mean drunk! Let me tell you what I think happened to him. I think he got a taste of the bright lights and big city and just never came back. Oh, Lord! Won't there be a reckoning for that man!"

Mr. Glasby roughly cleared his throat. The gesture snapped the woman out of her gossip trance.

"Oh, mercy me! But don't I go on! Let me help you put together your Christmas. Do you have a budget, Jasper?" she asked, a bit red-faced.

"No, ma'am. I just want to make it nice. We're gonna need the works. I'll trust you for the proper guidance," said Jasper, smiling.

The men turned back to each other and resumed their conversation on the foolish notion of prohibition.

"Very well, Jasper. Let me gather you up a proper Christmas dinner!" said Mrs. Glasby, bubbling out from behind the counter.

"Oh, ma'am, if you could put enough groceries together for not only Christmas but for the next week or two, I'd be much appreciative," added Jasper.

"Oh, but what a Christmas ya'll are gonna have!" she said, beaming. She ran to the back and returned with a brand new Red Rider wagon in tow. As she passed the other gentleman, she snatched Mr. Glasby's cup and downed it in one swallow. Mr. Glasby tried to look gruff but could not contain a smile. The other men joined in with laughter.

"Tis the Season to be Jolly . . ." sang Mrs. Glasby, as she loaded the toy wagon.

"Jasper," said Mr. Glasby.

"Yes, sir?"

"Do you have a means of delivering these goods?"

The other men smiled and waited for his response.

"Well, I hadn't planned that far ahead," answered Jasper, looking down at his shoes and starting to fidget.

Mr. Glasby could see Jasper was getting a little uncomfortable conversing but was trying hard not to show it. By now, many folks in town were aware that Jasper just didn't speak much.

"Let me tell you what, son. We'll keep your goods here tonight. Tomorrow morning, say around nine,

I'll bring around the Ford, and we'll deliver them together, snow be damned!"

"Mr. Glasby!" said Mrs. Glasby, popping her head around the corner.

"Sorry, Mother, must be the whiskey talking," said Mr. Glasby, as if he'd said it a thousand times.

She gave him a last scolding glance and carried on with her caroling.

"As a matter of fact, you just head on home and get a fire going. When you come back in the morning, we'll square up," said Mr. Glasby, refilling his own cup with a little less coffee and a little more Christmas cheer.

Jasper was overwhelmed. He reverently removed his hat and could only manage, "I'm much obliged, Mr. Glasby. Merry Christmas, sir."

"Merry Christmas, Jasper. We'll see ya in the morning."

"Nine o'clock, sharp!" said Jasper.

"Well, thereabouts," smiled Mr. Glasby, lifting his cup.

"Merry Christmas, Mrs. Glasby!" called Jasper.

"Merry Christmas, Jasper!" he heard from the back of the store.

When Jasper stepped out of the store, dusk had taken over. Shimmering pale blue light reflected off the blanketing snow. There wasn't a soul stirring; for the moment, the streets were his. No snow was falling at the time, but the sweet smell of moisture coming in with the north wind was foreboding. More snow was on its way. "Lord have mercy, ain't it cold? It's got to be single digits," he thought to himself.

Upon entering his house, Jasper did not take time to remove his boots, or even his hat. He walked straight to the kitchen and sat by the stove until he warmed up. He thought a cup of coffee was in order. The pump outside had been frozen up for a long time, so he stepped out the door, scooped up a bucket of snow and placed it on the stove.

CHAPTER XVIII
Christmas Day

Jasper was alone in front of Glasby's Hardware, nervously pacing back and forth. Six more inches of snow had fallen overnight. He pulled back his sleeve and looked at his Tip-Top wristwatch. It was 8:59. He so wanted the day to be special, and now it might not start at all. Could Mr. Glasby's Model T make it in the two feet of snow? Jasper took another look at his watch: 9:01.

"Land sakes!" said Jasper aloud.

Just then he heard a motor rumbling nearby. Down two blocks on Highway 81, he saw a black automobile turning towards him on Main. The waving arm from the driver's side told him it was Mr. Glasby. A rush of relief washed over Jasper. He returned the wave.

"Merry Christmas, Jasper!"

"Merry Christmas, Mr. Glasby!" shouted Jasper.

Mr. Glasby stopped in front of the store. The back tires on the Model T were covered with straw and wrapped with hemp rope. Jasper was impressed.

"Did you keep warm enough last night?" asked Mr. Glasby.

"I had the stove glowing red. It was just enough," said Jasper.

"I swear! I've been here going on twenty years and never seen more snow on Christmas," said Mr. Glasby.

"Yes, sir. Seems like it's always cold and dry. Did you have much trouble this morning?" asked Jasper.

"None at all, son. Let's get you loaded up," Mr. Glasby replied, unlocking the front door.

"Yes, sir."

Mr. Glasby entered the shop, walked to the back, and quickly emerged with the Red Rider Wagon Mrs. Glasby had packed the day before. It overflowed with canned and dry goods, including corn, peas, and candied yams. Half the wagon was filled with a ten-pound cured ham. Jasper's heart swelled; he could barely contain his excitement.

"Go ahead and load this up, Jasper. I'll be right back."

As Jasper loaded the car, he noticed a pecan pie in the front seat. Mr. Glasby approached with yet another wagon.

"Load up this wagon too, son. Both are presents for the children," he said.

Jasper froze. He knew he had the money to pay, but this might add up to fifteen or twenty dollars! Well, that was just fine.

"Lord have mercy," said Jasper as he surveyed the second wagon, packed with bags of flour, sugar, and cornmeal.

When the men finished loading the car, Jasper reached for his money, but Mr. Glasby stopped him.

"This here's from me and the Mrs., for you and that young family. Oh yeah, she also made a pie for ya'll and told me to tell you, 'May God bless you all on this glorious day!'"

"I don't know what to say, Mr. Glasby," said Jasper.

"Just say, 'Merry Christmas,' son, and don't for a second think you owe us, or you don't deserve this. You're living proof every child born is a blessing. Let's make this a day these children won't forget!"

Jasper couldn't speak. The amazing gesture silenced him. He shook Mr. Glasby's hand, got into the passenger seat, and steadied the pecan pie on his lap. The Christmas spirit beamed from the men on the short drive to the Menders' home.

With a gentle sputter and bang, the automobile rolled to a quiet stop in front of the house. For a moment, the thick blanket of snow hushed everything, but only for a moment.

"Jasper!!!!! Merry Christmas, Jasper!!!!" Betty and Freddy came roaring out the front door in their pajamas and shoes. Jasper and Mr. Glasby got out of the car and waited for the children.

"Freddy! Betty! Ya'll get right back in this house before you catch your death of cold!" shouted Evelynn from the front porch. As with all good mothers, she seamlessly switched from being a tough parent to a friendly hostess, greeting the men warmly.

"Merry Christmas," she said to them. Both men smiled and waved.

"Merry Christmas, Mrs. Mender," said Mr. Glasby. Jasper was still finding it difficult to speak. The joy in his heart filled all his emotions. Evelynn's eyes widened as she saw the holiday bounty being unloaded.

"What in the world have you done, Jasper Whittington?" asked Evelynn, watching the men.

"Don't thank me," said Jasper, finally finding his voice. The response froze Mr. Glasby for a moment.

"It was Santa Claus," Jasper said, winking at Mr. Glasby.

"Yay!!!" cried the children from the front door.

Freddy and Betty giggled as the men loaded up the two brand-new Red Rider Wagons and maneuvered them through the deep, virgin snow. There was a spill or two on the way to the porch, but none the worse for wear. After getting them on the porch, Evelynn called the children, "Ya'll get out here and take all this to the kitchen."

"Yes, ma'am!" said Betty.

"Ya'll come on in out of the weather and warm up!" said Evelynn.

"Thank you, Mrs. Mender, but as the lowest-ranking member of the Glasby kitchen, my duties are to assist in the day's festivities while avoiding as much responsibility as possible," politely answered Mr. Glasby. "I must report back to the Mrs."

"Please pass on our season's greetings to her," said Evelynn, absolutely beaming with the Christmas spirit.

Mr. Glasby reached into his coat, pulled out a half-pint of whiskey, and offered it to Jasper. With just a glance, both men saw Evelynn's eyes change from joyous to fearful as she slipped into bad memories.

Jasper held up his hand and said, "That's very generous, but I'll pass. I need to save the room in my belly for ham and pie." All three laughed, and the joy came back to Evelynn's eyes. Mr. Glasby smiled, tipped his hat, and said, "I must return to my assigned duties, or Mrs. Glasby's next chore will be skinning me and tacking my hide on the west wall to dry! May you all have a wonderful, magical day, and give those children of yours a hug and kiss from the Glasby household."

"Merry Christmas, Mr. Glasby! God Bless," said Evelynn. She reached her arms around his neck and gently kissed him on the cheek.

"Yay!!!" cried the children, running to Mr. Glasby, hugging both his kneecaps.

A red-faced Mr. Glasby could only manage a smile and a tip of his hat. He turned and walked back to his Ford, feeling three feet off the ground. On the drive home, he wondered why this was the first Christmas they had done this. No matter. Next year would be bigger.

Returning to the warm kitchen, they heard a distant train whistle.

"Ya'll come back out here and watch this!" said Jasper.

In moments, they could hear the steam engine chugging. Though the snow was deep, and despite Christmas, the trains still ran. The 10:10 from Chickasha was on time. The plowed snow was thrown a hundred yards on both sides of the track. Some even landed on the roof of their house! Slack-jawed and eyes wide open, the children were overwhelmed by the mighty sight.

"Alright, children! Get in that house and warm up. We'll get Christmas dinner going!" said Evelynn, trying to keep some semblance of order.

Evelynn sorted the goods. What a feast! Why, that ham will last weeks, she thought. There were white potatoes, red potatoes, yellow squash, and collard greens, several cans of corn and green beans, and Lord have mercy; what in the world was this? Canned mackerel? As Evelynn unpacked, the children changed into warm, dry clothes, then returned to the kitchen.

Jasper called to them, "Feddy, Betty, listen up. These Red Riders came straight from the North Pole! Santa brought them just for you. Now, before ya'll go rearin' and tearin', let your Mama go over the rules and where you can play with them, OK?"

The children's shoulders went a bit slack, and they answered in unison, "Yes, sir."

"Go ahead and take them to the front room for now. But don't you dare hit a wall or a stick of furniture," instructed Evelynn. Barely containing themselves, they carefully took their wagons to the living room.

"Evelynn, how may I help?" asked Jasper.

"Just have a seat at the table. I'll get a pot of coffee going," she said.

"Well, at least let me . . ."

"Now, hush with that and sit," Evelynn cut him off with a smile.

Somehow, the mild scolding seemed affectionate and warmed his heart.

Knock, knock, knock! Sounded from the front door. Jasper stood and imagined Mr. Glasby must have missed something in the backseat.

"I'll get it," said Jasper.

When he opened the door, he found not Mr. Glasby but a lanky, dingy man with bright green eyes and a toothless grin.

"Why, Koen Van Haaften! Well, get in here before you freeze!" said Jasper.

Koen stepped in, and Jasper closed the door. The men embraced. Koen looked as shaggy as ever and had gone a little grayer. The joy in both men's faces was unmistakable. They were happy to see each other.

Freddy ran to the men and asked, "Is that Santa?"

They laughed at the question. Jasper answered, "No, Freddy. This is Mr. Koen Van Haaften. His grandaddy came from Holland, but he don't have no wooden shoes!"

"Wooden shoes?" asked Freddy, with deep curiosity.

"That's right! When my grandaddy's feet caught a chill, why he'd just chop down a tree and carve him out some shoes!" said Koen.

The children fell silent. The revelation of wooden shoes boggled their minds.

Evelynn stood at the kitchen door quietly watching the two exchange pleasantries. Jasper followed Koen's gaze toward her.

"Oh! Mrs. Evelynn Mender, please meet, Mr. Koen Van Haaften. Koen, Mrs. Evelynn Mender."

"Merry Christmas, Mr. Van Haaften. Welcome to our home. Please join us in the kitchen," said Evelynn. She was still aglow from the Christmas surprise, and her radiance took Koen aback.

He removed his hat and only managed, "Much obliged, ma'am."

As the adults headed to the kitchen, the young ones called an emergency meeting to quietly discuss their options now that they had wagons. Should they make a wagon train to head out and settle the Wild, Wild West? They could start a new railway system delivering products and dry goods to the kitchen from the far reaches of China. This was going to be a serious meeting, indeed!

"Coffee, Mr. Van Haaften?" asked Evelynn as she quietly sized him up.

"Yes, ma'am, Mrs. Mender. And please, call me Koen."

"And please, call me Evelynn," she said smiling.

The sun momentarily broke through the clouds. Bright sunlight reflected from the fresh snow and beamed through the kitchen windows, giving the table a heavenly radiance. Evelynn brought the coffee pot from the stove with a cup for Koen.

"This is quite a surprise, Koen. I imagined you sitting under a palm tree, drinking from a coconut in sunny California. Did you miss the weather here?" asked Jasper. Evelynn and Koen laughed at the question.

"Not so much," Koen said with a smile. "I'd been working on the same produce farm in San Fernando since I headed out there in '15. It was old Boswell Thomas's place. He just lost his wife, and his children were grown and moved on.

He picked up me and a couple of Mexican families who were camped near the station. He had some small houses on his land so he put us up and we worked for him, taking care of a few orchards, peaches and plums mostly. He kept us fed and clothed, and we lived rent-free. Once a month or so he'd give us a little "walking around" money. He was a proper, kind man. He even tried sending them Mexican kids to school. But the schools wouldn't have them. So he taught the kids and me some reading, writing, and a little ciphering.

Well, the good Lord called Mr. Thomas last month. He was in church. He bowed his head for benediction, closed his eyes, and they never opened again. Within a few days, the sheriff came out to the farm and told all of us we had no right to be there. He said we needed to pack up and get gone by sundown. Well, them families headed back to Mexico, which left me alone, and Hell, I ain't got kin nowhere!"

"Hell!" shouted Freddy from the front room. Both kids giggled.

"Excuse me, ma'am, I need to be more mindful of my language," said Koen.

Evelynn smiled and nodded. Koen continued.

"Well, then I thought about Jasper P. Whittington III. The Louisville Kid!"

"Louisville Kid?" cried Betty, running into the kitchen. "Were you a real live cowboy, Jasper?"

"No, sugar. That's just where Mr. Van Hafften and I met," said Jasper.

"Did ya'll meet in a rootin', tootin' saloon, Mr. Van Haaften?" asked Freddy

"Naw, son. We met in ja . . ." A look from Jasper shushed Koen.

"That's a story for another day," finished Koen.

"What's the P stand for, Jasper?" asked Evelynn.

"Nothing, just P. I grew up in an orphanage. Just got dropped off there. That's the name pinned on the basket I was in," said Jasper.

"So you have no idea who the first or second are either?" she asked.

"No, ma'am," said Jasper. The two men quietly relived the run-in at Ada. Evelynn sensed there was more to the story but let it be.

"Jasper, do you have running water at your house?" asked Evelynn.

"No, the last few days I've been melting buckets of snow on the cook stove," he said.

"Well, do you have a wash tub?" she asked. The question silenced Jasper for a moment, and then he caught a good whiff of Koen.

"Yes, I do," said Jasper.

"Excuse me just a moment, gentlemen," said Evelynn, rising from the table.

"How was your trip from California, Koen?" asked Jasper.

"Oh, fine. I had money for a ticket, so I kept warm for most of the trip, except heading through the Rockies. The snow was so deep it slowed the train. And it was damn cold!" said Koen.

"Damn!" shouted Freddy and Betty from the other room, which did not escape Mom's ears, standing at the kitchen door, holding fresh clothes for Koen. She gave her new acquaintance a fierce, motherly stare.

"Pardon me, Miss Evelynn," said Koen. He quickly crumbled under her glare. His sincere regret softened her heart, and she let it go with a smile.

"Here's some fresh clothes, Koen," said Evelynn, handing him overalls, long johns, a shirt, and socks.

"Ya'll go to Jasper's and get cleaned up. Food's on its way!"

At first, Koen looked confused. Then he realized he hadn't even stood near a bar of soap since spring.

"Children! Come to the kitchen," said the young mother. "Jasper and Koen will be back in a little bit. They're going to get cleaned up at Jasper's house. Now, tell them what you'll do until they come back."

"Be-have!" the two said. Their smiles stole the hearts of everyone in the room.

The men headed out.

The clouds closed and blocked the sun again, returning the day to a mournful grey. They gingerly maneuvered with high steps until they reached Jasper's home, just two blocks away. Once again, the home was cold.

Jasper opened the door and said, "Don't worry about your shoes. Just get in the kitchen, and I'll get this place warmed up!"

The men hurried to the stove where some low-glowing embers were still present, and Jasper stoked up a fire. He grabbed the bucket, went outside, and scooped up snow to fill the number six washtub just out the backdoor. He called for Koen to give him a hand carrying the tub back to the hot stove. The two sat at the kitchen table, both amazed to see their paths cross again.

"I can't tell you how happy I am to see you, Koen, but how'd you find me?" asked Jasper.

"I know'd you was in Marlow. It just seemed like a good fit for you, and Marlow is such a small town I figured I just needed to ask around and someone would know where you was living. It'd be just a matter of time. Then, as the train was pulling into the station I was looking out the window of the car, and I seen ya'll standing on the front porch. I don't mind telling you, I thought my eyes had gone caddywhompus! But sure enough, there you stood," said Koen.

"I truly believed I'd never see you again. I thought you'd hung your hat in California for good," Jasper said.

"Oh, I was happy there. Them Mexican folks done took me in as one of theirs. The kids called me 'Tio'. That means uncle in Mexican. When they took off to Mexico, they wanted me to go with them, and I sure enough had a hankering to. But then I figured the next place I stop, I'm a stayin'. And spending the rest of my days wondering how you was a doing and not knowing, well, that just wouldn't do. Oh, I figured you'd be alright but, shit fire to save matches, son! You settled in AND got a sweetheart too!" Koen exclaimed.

"She ain't my sweetheart," said Jasper. Koen stared at him blankly, then smiled.

"She's sweet on you, too. I can tell."

"Well, that don't matter none on account of she's married," said Jasper.

"What in tarnation are you doing with a married woman, Jasper?" asked Koen.

"It ain't like that, Koen. Yesterday, Freddy got a marble stuck in his windpipe. Evelynn screamed for help and I happened to be walking by. After helping the boy spit out that marble and half his breakfast, she invited me by for Christmas. I pretty much keep to myself, but I thought it'd be nice to spend the holiday with a real family. Besides, I have me a steady income and don't hardly spend it on anything. So I thought I'd give them kids a proper Christmas."

"Who owns this here house?" asked Koen.

"I do. Bought and paid for," said Jasper.

After a long pause, Koen asked, "You ain't one of them rich eccentrics, are you?"

Jasper broke out with laughter from Koen's suddenly expanding vocabulary.

"No. Shortly after you took off to California, I took up work with the local funeral director. Just like you, his patience and charity put me on the right path. I was his only friend when he died, so he took care of me in his will."

"So, you're all set up?" asked Koen.

"Nope! We're all set up, Koen. Now that you're back in Oklahoma, we can get you established too. You know, it's pretty nice here, apart from an occasional snowfall." Both men laughed. Jasper continued, "You can stay in this house as long as you'd like. Maybe even find some work."

"Now looky here, Jasper. I didn't come for no free ride. I can take care of myself," said a slightly bewildered Koen.

"I know that, Koen. Better than anyone else, I reckon!" Jasper paused for awhile, then asked, "Did you ever hear, 'You reap what you sow'?"

"Well, sure," said Koen.

"That torpedo attack had me tied up in knots. I couldn't talk, couldn't sleep. I thought everyone saw me as crazy. I was in a terrible way, and it didn't look like it would end well. Then I met you. Not only did you keep me off the gallows, but you gave me hope in your own odd way." Jasper moved in closer. "You earned this; you belong here."

Koen looked long and hard at the floor between his knees. It really wasn't charity, he thought. He reckoned they were just a team, that's all! Koen was feeling a little overwhelmed. He could only say, "Let me get washed off, and we'll get us a Christmas meal."

"All right, now," said Jasper, patting him on his back and leaving the room.

Within twenty minutes, the two were back high-stepping in the deep snow.

"What happened to her old man?" asked Koen.

"Her husband went missing after the war, and she hasn't heard a peep from him in over five years. Oh, and by the way, there will be no drinking around her and them children. He must have been an ornery drunk cause she's mighty touchy about it. That doesn't make any difference to me anyhow. I stopped drinking," said Jasper.

"You don't drink no more?" asked Koen, almost reverently.

"Nope!" answered Jasper, withholding the fact that the decision was made only about an hour back.

Koen stopped walking to take in Jasper's words. He remembered a few men who couldn't handle their drink. They all seemed to end up hidden and alone, like they were in an unmarked grave, forgotten. Koen drank to reward himself. He drank because it made him a better storyteller, not because he needed it. Jasper drank 'cause he was all torn up on the inside. Seemed he couldn't function without it. "But now he's found his peace," thought Koen. Shit, Koen couldn't remember the last day he didn't have a drink. But he could see Jasper was committed to this; so after a brief ponderance, Koen nodded and said, "Well, I reckon I don't drink neither. Besides, it's against the law now!"

Both men laughed. "I don't know about you, but I'd prefer to stay outta them drunk tanks. I'm getting too old for that mess," said Koen.

Before the men entered the yard on Nabor Street, they could smell heavenly aromas billowing from Evelynn's kitchen. Their bellies tugged and rumbled in response. Their legs responded to their stomachs by picking up the pace.

Within a minute, the gentlemen stood at the front door, hats in hand. Evelynn opened the door with a smile. From the living room they heard a loud reenactment of "Hopalong Cassidy" chasing down "Black Bart." Freddy thought his talents were wasted on playing a supporting role, the bad guy who'll die in the end, but he still gave it his best.

"Pew-pew!"

"Bang! Bang! Bang!"

The deadly exchange continued as Freddy and Betty rolled by the open door, not acknowledging the newly arrived audience. The three adults carefully maneuvered themselves around the ongoing gun battle and almost made it through unscathed until Black Bart fell out of character and began shouting, "Santa! Santa!" Knee hugs and season's greetings ensued.

"Ya'll must be starving! Come and sit at the table while I finish up," said Evelynn.

A baking dish filled with steaming, candied yams sat next to a bowl of green beans and a cornbread casserole. Evelynn was at the stove, searing ham steaks in a cast iron skillet, and you could smell the dinner rolls baking in the oven.

"Freddy! Betty! Ya'll put away those wagons and clean up for Christmas dinner," said Evelynn.

Freddy was lying on the parlor floor, unresponsive. Black Bart had taken one right between the eyes!

"Better not set a plate for Black Bart! I reckon he's pushing up daisies!" shouted Betty.

"Oh! I'm fine. I've done got doctored up!" said Freddy, jumping to his feet and displaying a miraculous recovery.

The grown-ups all laughed. Jasper was looking forward to watching Koen watch Freddy eat.

Freddy and Betty came running into the kitchen with clean hands and faces. They both stopped in their tracks when they realized only one empty seat was left at the table. Freddy dashed to Jasper's lap and snuggled in.

"Freddy!" said Evelynn with a disapproving tone.

"Oh, he's fine. You might need to throw a tarp over me, though," said Jasper.

Evelynn glared at Freddy, put one hand on her hip, and pointed a dripping wooden spoon at him. Without a single word from her, Freddy said, "Behave!" She gave him a stern but approving nod and pulled the bread out of the stove.

The table was set, and Lord, what a table!

"Blessing! Blessing!" said Betty.

"I want Santa to say the blessing!" said Freddy.

"Santa! Santa!" chanted the children.

Evelynn asked Koen, "As our new guest, Mr. Van Haaften, would you bless our food?"

Koen was overwhelmed. She was aglow with the holiday spirit, and he could not refuse. Everyone joined hands and bowed their heads, then awaited Koen's blessing. After an uncomfortably long silence, Koen prayed.

"Lord? I know'd it's been a while since you last heard from me. Most of the time, when you hear from me, I'm knee-deep in sh...shtuff. But sitting here in this company with these vittles, all I got to say is thank you. Thank you for bringing us all together at this particular place and this particular time. Thank you for looking out for my friend, Jasper, and this here family. If it be your will, let's make it the first of many holidays spent together. It just seems like this is where we all belong. Though it don't seem right, I'd still like to ask you a favor, Lord. Since you done took Mr. Thomas into your bosom, could you look out for the Melendez family down in Mexico? I sure enough miss them folks and I would be much appreciative if you could. And one more thing, Lord, if you wouldn't mind. Don't let that rascal Freddy eat up all them dinner rolls before I get mine! Amen!"

The kids giggled, and the grown-ups smiled and repeated, "Amen!" The superb dinner was also served with entertainment! Freddy gave his interpretation of a lion ripping apart a zebra carcass, much to the amazement of Koen and the chagrin of the always manners-mindful Betty. As Koen requested in his blessing, this was the first of many holidays they would spend together as a family.

ABOUT THE AUTHOR

Jon West

Jon West, born and raised in southwest Oklahoma, discovered his passion for storytelling at an early age. Immersed in the tales of ghosts, frontier life, and family adventures shared by the elders of his close-knit community, he developed a rich imagination and a love for crafting narratives. Solitude often became a source of creative inspiration, nurturing his talent for storytelling.

Jon's perspective broadened during his decade-long military service in Europe. The camaraderie of service life and the vibrant cultures he experienced left a lasting impact, enriching his storytelling with depth and authenticity.

Now retired and living in San Antonio, Jon enjoys a fulfilling life as a grandfather, finding joy in family, love, and a renewed dedication to the arts. Alongside his wife and creative partner, Amanda, he has embraced writing as his chosen form of expression.

Drawing from a lifetime of diverse experiences—from the wide-open landscapes of Oklahoma to the bustling streets of Madrid—Jon crafts stories that blend sincerity and imagination. While he may indulge in occasional embellishments, his work remains firmly rooted in passion, truth, and a profound respect for the art of storytelling.

Made in the USA
Monee, IL
20 March 2025